The Venetian

D1665789

Copyright © 2014 by Lina Ellina

All rights reserved. Published by Armida Publications Ltd.

No part of this publication may be reproduced, stored in a retrieval system,
or transmitted in any form or by any means, electronic, mechanical,
photocopying, recording, or otherwise, without permission of the publisher.
For information regarding permission, write to
Armida Publications Ltd, P.O.Box 27717, 2432 Engomi, Nicosia, Cyprus
or email: info@armidapublications.com

Armida Publications is a founding member
of the Association of Cypriot Book Publishers,
and a member of the Independent Book Publishers Association (USA)

www.armidabooks.com | Great Literature. One Book At A Time.

Summary:
A Renaissance-era mystery unravels through the deft fingertips
of debut author Lina Ellina in this story-within-a story,
linking present day characters to history's most romantic intrigues.

A king's wedding and a present day chef's holiday are interwoven beautifully
as details emerge about an intergenerational connection as delicate and rare
as the Italian and Cypriot landscapes that form the backdrop
for this literary rumination on life, love, food, and fellowship.

[1. General - Fiction 2. Literary - Fiction 3. Historical - Fiction
4. Romance - Contemporary 5. Romance - Historical
6. Romance - Time Travel 7. Travel - Literary]

Editing:
Miriam Pirolo

Cover image:
Portrait of a Young Man (detail) by Sandro Botticelli

This novel is a work of fiction.
Any resemblance to real people, living or dead, is entirely coincidental.

1st edition: April 2012
2nd edition: April 2014

ISBN-13 (paperback): 978-9963-706-98-3

Book and cover design by Armida

The Venetian

Lina Ellina

ARMIDA

To my husband Andreas,

who has given me wings,

and our wonderful children

ACKNOWLEDGEMENTS

I would like to thank the following
for their invaluable advice and help with this book:
Maria Carlino, Anna Saif, Milena Furini, Dr Nicholas Coureas

Medieval times in Cyprus is an extended period particularly significant to the evolution of the country, playing an important role in the island's history, traditions, culture and interrelations with Europe.

The history, legends and oral testimonies of the period, still hold the interest of scientific researchers and scholars, intrigue the creativeness of writers and poets, and appeal to the imagination of every day individuals. The existing important monuments stand out like vigilant guards of a heritage not yet fully recorded and, to date, its depth and significance not yet fully revealed.

Therefore, it was a pleasant surprise when Lina Ellina was kind enough to entrust me with a first reading and request for a forward for her novel "The Venetian".

This work is written in fluid and pleasant English. It is a novel that uses actual events and facts to unfold before us parallel human stories with great sensitivity and imagination.

With accuracy of description and narration, and in lyrical terms, the author analyzes characters, specifies actual places and locales, introduces historical documentation and includes elements of folkloric traditions. In this manner she succeeds in keeping the reader engaged until the very end.

After thoroughly studying all aspects of life in Medieval Cyprus, Lina Ellina proceeds to create an excellent novel where myth and fact are skillfully interwoven and developed. It is a novel that takes us to familiar landmarks where we encounter people close to us, persons who we feel have lived in the past and are still among us.

ANDREAS CHRISTOU

MAYOR OF LIMASSOL

The Venetian explores the similarities that unite two peoples of the Mediterranean, the Italians and the Cypriots, both in the Middle Ages and in contemporary times.

With sensitivity and eloquence, Lina Ellina looks deeply into the soul of her protagonists, as she narrates their human concerns, interwoven with the developments of their time, customs, and traditions which depict both periods in detail.

The Venetian will not only thrill the reader with the accuracy of the historical research that allows us to take a peak in time, in people's everyday life, but at the same time, it serves as a culinary guide to the island's flavors.

It is Lina's spiritual richness that comes out – a woman who has the smile as a basic element of her face, sensitivity as a quality in her relation with others, and love for other nations, reflected by the many languages she speaks. Positive energy in a sea of negative energy, certainly nourished by her life partner, the extraordinary Andreas.

The Venetian is an imaginary journey that brings two far-off lands together, an imaginary journey and a story one surely has to read and remember.

GUGLIELMO BRUSCO

VICE-PRESIDENT OF ROVIGO

PREFACE

The Lusignan Period[1] (1192-1489) was perhaps Cyprus' most illustrious epoch. An island rich in resources, at the crossroads of three continents between Occident and Orient, Cyprus was one of the most popular meeting places for trading European products for those from the East - especially during the papal embargo that prohibited Christians from trading in Muslim ports. As one Christian stronghold after another fell into Muslim hands in the Eastern Mediterranean basin, the kingdom of Cyprus attained an unprecedented position of influence and importance, given its small size, particularly during the first two hundred years of the Lusignan dynasty. Cypriots, the majority of whom were degraded to serfdom, however, had little - if any - share in the newfound prosperity.

When in 1367, Peter I, the King of Jerusalem, Cyprus, and Armenia, made a tour through European capitals in search of support against the looming hazard of a massive military offensive by the Muslims, his fellow sovereigns accepted him with honors but provided no useful aide. The Doge of Venice, Marco Cornaro, and his very wealthy cousin, Federico, privately funded the king's request. This move redounded to their acquiring rich estates in the Episkopi peninsula, near Limassol[2], along the south coast of the island. It also inaugurated a long-lasting relationship between the Cornaro and the Lusignan families. It was a twist of fate, perhaps, that the last monarch in the Lusignan dynasty was not a Frank per se but a Venetian who bore the name of Cornaro.

---

1 After almost nine centuries of Byzantine Rule, Richard the Lionheart conquered Cyprus in 1191 and sold it to the Templar Knights. Unable to rule the island, they sold it back to Richard who then sold it to Guy de Lusignan, of Poitiers, France, in 1192.

2 The Frankish name for Lemesos.

With the loss of Famagusta[3], the mainstay of the island's economy[4], to the Genoese and the Mameluke[5] attacks that resulted in an annual tribute[6] to the Sultan of Egypt and drained the kingdom's treasury, Lusignan's ability to exercise control over all aspects of public life declined rapidly in the fifteenth century. The highlight of John II's reign (1432-1458), which was marked by dissension and intrigue, was his marriage to Elena Palaeologina, the Byzantine emperor's granddaughter. Queen Elena, a great heroine for the Cypriots and a dangerous enemy of the Franks, was stronger in character than her husband and took over the management of the kingdom, bringing Greek Orthodox faith and culture out of the oblivion in which it had languished after centuries of persecution.

In 1456, their daughter, Princess Charlotte, married Prince John of Coimbra who had been chosen by the Latin Church as Queen Elena's rival. Friction soon broke out, and the prince took his wife away from the palace. Forthwith, the Knights Hospitaller, religious enemies of the queen, rebelled against her, causing fractious incidents in Nicosia that escalated into a violent affray. In reprisal, the queen's trusted Royal Chamberlain incited the people to rise up against the prince, who was found dead a few days later. Seeking vengeance, Charlotte turned to her half-brother James, the king's illegitimate son with Marietta from Patras, for assistance. James, who was only seventeen at the time and already the titular Archbishop of Nicosia, murdered the Royal Chamberlain. In an effort to repress potential uprisings and restore peace, the king deprived his son of the archbishopric. Fearing the queen's rage, James absconded to Rhodes only to return five months later and kill several of his enemies in one night.

---

3 The Frankish name for Ammohostos, meaning hidden in the sand – in 1374.

4 'It is the richest of all cities and her citizens are the richest of men.' (Ludolf von Suchen, De Terra Sancta, 1336) Indicative of its wealth was testimony that merchants' daughters wore more jewels than kings at their coronations.

5 Military caste in Muslim societies.

6 In 1426.

In 1458, both the queen and the king died within three months of each other, and Charlotte ascended the throne. James swore allegiance to his half-sister, but his enemies persuaded the queen that he was conniving to assassinate her. Fearing for his life, James fled to the Sultan of Egypt, a move that was interpreted as an imminent threat by the nobles in Charlotte's Court. In 1459, Charlotte married the Duke of Savoy, and envoys were sent to the sultan to ensure his support. The sultan, however, decided in favor of James who returned to Cyprus followed by supporters and Mamelukes. People's approval constantly grew, and soon, only Kyreneia, Charlotte's seat, and Famagusta, ruled by the Genoese, resisted him. Charlotte fled Cyprus in quest of allies; nevertheless, her endeavors were to no avail. Eventually, Kyreneia capitulated in 1463.

When Andrea Cornaro, the Doge's grandson, was accused of an alleged election scam in 1457, Marco Cornaro failed to denounce his younger brother, and the two were banished to Cyprus. On the one hand, this gave them the opportunity to fully devote themselves to their family enterprises and multiply their wealth. On the other hand, they were flirting with disgrace, and Marco's political career was bruised. In the war of succession following the death of King John II, the Cornaro brothers shifted their aid from the lawful heiress to the king's illegitimate son.

In 1464, James drove the Genoese out of Famagusta and united the whole island once again into a single kingdom. His prevailing was partly due to Andrea Cornaro's support. In return, the young king appointed the preeminent Venetian patrician, who acted as his banker, his counselor and Auditor of the Kingdom. Notwithstanding his becoming the unquestionable ruler of Cyprus, the crown felt heavy on the young king's head. With the threat of an invasion by the Ottoman Turks hanging over his kingdom like the sword of Damocles, James II, or the Bastard, promptly recognized the urgent need for a strong alliance. Marriage appeared to be an attractive means to this end.

The Cornaro brothers had great plans for the king's marriage and their own future, but very few men in Venice were let in on them. Cavalier Marco Cornaro's trusty friend and cousin, Captain Alexandro Zanetti, was one of them. With Andrea now in Nicosia[7] and Marco, who on occasions accomplished delicate diplomatic missions on behalf of the new king, back in Venice, and the recent death of their estate supervisor, the two brothers saw the need for a trustworthy man to run their family sugar mill and their large estates in their absence. They originally thought they had found this man in the person of their loyal cousin Alexandro, but he persuaded them to place their faith in his son Marin who would be equally devoted to them. What he might have lacked in experience, he would make up for with his enterprising spirit and diligence.

---

7 The Frankish name for Lefkosia.

I

VENICE, *1467*

Marin had a sleepless night anticipating the world of adventure that awaited him at dawn. His father, captain of a commercial galley and distant cousin of Cavaliers Marco and Andrea Corner, or better known in history as Cornaro, had arranged for twenty-one-year-old Marin to join Andrea in Cyprus. The young man had been traveling with the captain for several years now, but this voyage would be like no other. A new life full of prospects lay ahead if he were vigilant and scrupulous. His father's words 'Anything's possible if you use your brain and work hard' echoed in his ears.

At the first light of dawn, Marin put on his white wide-sleeved, low neckline linen shirt that was decorated with embroidery. He put on his hip-length tight-fitting Glaucous blue doublet that matched the color of his eyes. It belted at the waist, giving the impression of a short skirt below which was fashionable among the young men of his time. Its sleeves were full and puffy. Wearing a self-satisfied grin, he looked in the mirror at the long attenuated appearance his tight hose and thigh-boots gave him and smoothed his jet-black hair. Marin's good looks had often won him young women's affection in all ports of call.

He closed his trunk, donned his short gown, and picked up his hat. He cast one last glance around his chamber and looked out the window at the torrent and the lightning that lit up the threatening dark grey January sky for a fleeting moment. The water had risen perilously, and Venice seemed to be once more on the threshold of a deluge.

He told his servant to carry his trunk along with his father's to the gondola tied up in the canal outside the house and slid into a seat at the breakfast table in the kitchen. He ignored the spicy ginger chicken and nibbled on some bread and Padua sausage, washing it down with some ale. His mother asked a female servant to wake the children to bid their father and their brother farewell and sat at the table. It was a brief breakfast where words were best left unspoken whenever they were sailing to faraway lands.

When Marin got up to leave the table, his mother walked up to him. The fringed sleeves of her long burgundy velvet dress swished as she put her arms around him. She hid her face on his chest and bravely fought back the tears in her eyes. She then lifted her head and kissed him on the forehead.

"Make me proud, Marin!"

It was not her place to tell her husband not to travel in this weather or to cry out that she didn't want her eldest son sent so far away from her. If there was anyone who understood her just by laying his eyes on her it was Marin. For years after giving birth to Marin, Anna Zanetti couldn't conceive, and she had fully devoted herself to the upbringing of her only child in the long periods of her husband's absence. She had no doubt that the captain, for whom she had the greatest esteem on account of his integrity, loved his wife, but he was a bit rough around the edges.

"Haven't I always?" Marin asked.

His mother nodded, and the young man offered her a tender smile. He hated to think how long it would take before he saw his mother again. So many thoughts and emotions he wanted to share with her, but now was not the time. Instead, he kissed her on both cheeks and stepped outside discreetly to give his parents some privacy for their parting.

The night before, he had inadvertently overheard his mother pleading with his father to search out a farm in the countryside. His mother had been asking her husband to settle down for some time now, but that was the first time his father had consented - even if vaguely. "Soon," flabbergasted Marin heard him promise. His father's love had been the sea, or so he thought.

Never had he envisioned the intrepid captain tied down to the land. The young man pondered how one's life can take an entirely different course on account of a single decision.

2

ROVIGO, 2010

Casually attired in his light khaki chino pants and steel blue dress shirt that matched his Glaucous blue eyes, Lorenzo Zanetti stretched his long, muscular legs, put one over the other, and flipped the page of *Il Gazettino di Rovigo* to the soft sound of Pavarotti's stentorian voice. He cast a quick glance at the blooming wisterias in the garden and then at the pendulum clock in the corner of the rustic kitchen as it chimed, and flashed a smile at Paola, his four-and-a-half-year-old daughter, who was just finishing her breakfast.

"Is my angel ready for kindergarten?"

"Yes, daddy. I'll go get my bag." The little wide-eyed girl with freckles and a lustrous golden-blonde ponytail climbed down the chair and removed her plate from the table.

"Run along now."

Lorenzo pushed his spectacles further up the bridge of his sculpted Roman nose and hid his chiseled face behind the newspaper once more. An article on the upcoming twinning of Comune di Rovigo in Italy with the Municipality of Famagusta[1] in Cyprus caught his attention. He had never been particularly interested in politics, but Famagusta, the stage for Shakespeare's Othello, had always been associated with the family legend of Marin Zanetti, the family benefactor, one of his enterprising ancestors in the fifteenth century, who had purportedly come into great wealth by doing business on the island.

"Come on, daddy. Let's go! I don't want to be late," Paola interrupted his thoughts a couple of minutes later. She was standing

---

1 The seat of the Municipality of Famagusta has been located in the free areas controlled by the Cyprus Government since 1974.

in the corridor with her arms folded in front of her chest, tapping her right foot, wondering what was taking him so long.

"Coming, angel."

Lorenzo removed his reading glasses and placed them on the coffee table next to him. He folded the newspaper, took one last sip of his cappuccino, and wetted his full lips. He grabbed his keys and his cell phone and had a look at his virile reflection and the touch of silver on his temples in the mirror, as he smoothed his thick jet-black hair that he kept neatly cut above his ears.

He took Paola by the hand and walked her to the car still thinking of his ancestor. He helped her with the child car seat and got behind the wheel. As he was steering the car onto the road, a bizarre idea sprang to mind. What if he were to search for Marin? His chance of finding his trail was probably one in a billion, but at least, the quest might add some spice to his otherwise monotonous life since Beth's tragic death.

3

LARNAKA INTERNATIONAL AIRPORT, 2010

"Cut. Again! I know you are tired. We all are, but smile, ladies, smile!" the director shooting a commercial said faking a smile, and the models dressed up as flight attendants walked past the check-in counters toward the cameras for the twentieth time that day.

In front of check-in counter 62, Madame Lanvin embraced Marina and kissed her three times in the usual French way. "So this is it! Goodbye, Marina, and thanks again for the wonderful tours. We truly enjoyed our stay in Cyprus."

Monsier Lanvin bent down to give five-foot-five Marina a farewell hug, too. "*Merci beaucoup*, Marina. You have made our vacation so memorable that we are thinking of coming back next year."

"That would be great," replied the young woman with the winsome, girlish face framed with rich dark brown curls. "I really wish we could meet again. I had a wonderful time, too... So I guess this is it then. Here's where I wish you a safe flight back home. Drop a line if you have time. I'd love to hear from you."

"*Mais, bien sûr!* And so should you. *Au revoir*, Marina."

"*Au revoir.*"

Marina straightened her fitted crimson blouse, the fashionable color of that spring, which lit up her facial features, and waited until their baggage was weighed and they went through passport control to ensure they wouldn't run into any difficulty. She waved at them one last time and headed back to the parking lot. A glance at her watch made her change her slow pace to brisk strides.

4

VENICE, 1467

When Alexandro Zanetti joined his son in the richly furnished living room, decorated with paintings by Lorenzetti's students, he was wearing his captain's face again. The young children of the family, two twin boys and two girls, came running down the stairs and stood in a straight line in front of the captain and Marin.

The twins, Zane and Lorenzo, shook their father's and brother's hand and with eyes glistening with enthusiasm, they wished them a safe journey. "We'll come and look you up soon, Marin. Father said he'll take us with him when summer comes," Zane, the elder twin by five minutes, announced somberly.

"I'll be waiting." Marin gave his brothers a hug. In the meantime, Maria and Sofia hid their faces in their father's arms and did their best not to look worried or sad.

"What do you want me to bring you when I come back? Silk perhaps to make fine new dresses?" the captain asked.

The girls locked eyes, turned to face their father, and said in unison, "Just come home safely."

Their father squeezed them tight and turned to the boys while Marin lifted up his sisters and planted a kiss on their foreheads. "Now, you be good girls and help *la mamma* with everything. Okay?"

"Yes, Marin. We'll miss you," they said unable to fight back their tears. They didn't have to be as brave with Marin as with their father.

"I'll miss you, too," Marin said with a lump in his throat.

"Boys, you know what to do," the captain said. "You are the

men of the house when we're gone, but always do as your mother says."

"Yes, captain," the boys replied grave faced.

The captain gave his wife one last hug, nodded decisively, and with agile movements, father and son strode to the gondola. As soon as they were out of sight, Marin's mother and the younger children lit a candle and said their prayers in front of the icon of the Madonna.

In the gondola, Marin focused his gaze on the multicolored arc of the rainbow, as sunrays shone on droplets of moisture, trying not to think of his mother and siblings. A few minutes later, they rowed by the stalls of the market outside the church of San Giovanni Elemosinario and the familiar smell of spices and oil perfumes penetrated his nostrils.

When he was a child, Marin would hang around fascinated by the liveliness of the potentially largest market in the world and the trading of a plethora of commodities from all parts of the then known world, most of which only the affluent bourgeois Venetians could afford. How many times had he imagined sailing the seas just like his father! When he was old enough to travel to the shores of the Eastern Mediterranean and the Near East, he was always heedful of merchandise he could trade. He had, in fact, managed to make a considerable profit based solely on his entrepreneurial instinct and street smartness.

The gondola floated under the wooden bridge that spanned the Grand Canal where barrels and boxes were unloaded on the banks into the *fondaci*[1].. Several men greeted his father respectfully as the gondola came to a halt at the docks. Marin's dream had been to become a galley captain one day, just like his father, but it looked as if a different path lay before him.

The two men mounted a galley with a high, carved prow deco-

---

1 The warehouses.

rated with a *miramare*², after which the vessel was named. The *Miramare* would usually lead a convoy of galleys carrying cargo and pilgrims to the Holy Land, but this time it would be a lonely voyage, as January and February were the months for repairs in the galleys and time for sailors with their families. Andrea Cornaro's request, however, was one that Captain Zanetti did not want to say 'no' to. Andrea needed Marin's assistance, yesterday if possible, as well as to move goods to and from Cyprus.

When all checks were carried out, the captain skillfully maneuvered the galley out of the lagoon, despite the wind gaining strength and the waves pounding on the docks, and sailed eastward. The captain's brief and precise orders were instantaneously carried out by his disciplined crew. The Venetians had been skilled seafarers for centuries.

When they were on the open sea, the young man took the golden St. Christopher hanging from the chain on his neck in his fingers. His mother had given it to him before he sailed on his first voyage, and it always filled him with comfort. The young Venetian mulled over his new assignment. Becoming Andrea Cornaro's right hand was a prestigious position, although he wasn't exactly sure what that entailed. Marin let his gaze rest on the horizon and vowed to see his mission through no matter what impediments lay ahead. His father had vouched for him.

---

2 A mermaid.

5

ROVIGO, *2010*

Lorenzo dropped Paola off, contemplating how Beth's death changed his life completely. He gave up his chef career at the Intercontinental Hotels chain and even refused an offer to work for *La Pergola,* a luxury three Michelin-starred restaurant in Rome. Instead, he opened up his own restaurant in his birthplace, Rovigo, a small and rather unknown town in Veneto, some eighty kilometers southwest of Venice, so as to offer Paola a child-friendly environment and to spend more time with her. He sold his modern apartment in Rome and bought a nice little villa with a beautiful garden not far from his sister's house, so that Paola could spend time with her six-year-old cousin Gianfranco. The two of them became inseparable from day one.

Rovigo's laid-back lifestyle slowed down his daily routine. In the mornings, Lorenzo would get up early, walk to the nearby market to pick fresh produce for his restaurant, come back home, make a healthy breakfast for Paola, and drive her to kindergarten. Afterward, he would go jogging and take a nap or take care of any of the day's business, pick up Paola from kindergarten, and spend the rest of the afternoon with her. She would then either spend the evening at his sister's playing with Gianfranco or 'help' him and his staff at the restaurant. Lorenzo had turned the tiny restaurant office into a bedroom, so that Paola could sleep until he was done working. He knew this arrangement was temporary. In fact, this was one of the issues that consumed a lot of his energy.

Location is essential for the success of a restaurant. Ca' Lorenzo was situated in the Piazza Vittorio Emanuele II, the heart of Rovigo and its Venetian background. The square serves as the most common meeting point, as it is surrounded by Palazzo Nodari, seat of the City Hall, Palazzo Roverella, famous for its temporary exhibitions, Palazzo Roncale, as well as the Accademia dei Concordi with its imposing library and the Gran Guardia, an impressive building used for conferences.

The sound of the car horn from the car behind him made him aware that the red traffic light had turned green. Lorenzo took a right turn and headed to the *piazza* and the registry office at the City Hall to get a *certificato di stato di famiglia*. This certificate, unique to Italy, records information on the entire family rather than just an individual. Lorenzo was relieved to find it empty.

"*Buon giorno!*" he said, approaching the counter.

The clerk raised his head and blinked at him. "*Buon giorno!*"

"I need a family certificate, please."

"Name and date of birth?" enquired the clerk behind the counter, returning his eyes to his desktop screen.

"Lorenzo Zanetti, January 23, 1975," he replied watching the diminutive figure push some keys on his keyboard.

"Did you know that alone in Rovigo, there are over four hundred people by the name of Zanetti?" The clerk observed Lorenzo's astonished face with amusement.

"Actually, I was hoping you might be able to help me trace an ancestor of mine. Marin Zanetti."

"When was he born?"

"Around the middle of the fifteenth century," Lorenzo replied tongue-tied.

"Well, this could be tricky." The clerk paused a moment and then said, "Our records date back to the first census in 1871."

"So these are the oldest records available?" Lorenzo asked rather disappointed.

"Let me think. Hmm…" He leaned back in his seat, rubbed

his chin contemplating for a while, and then said, "In 1563, re-
forms brought about by the Council of Trento required priests
to keep records of baptisms, marriages, and burials. In other
words, church records in Italy date back to the sixteenth century. For some cities, however," the clerk stopped again dramatically, "church records begin earlier - some even as early as the
fourteenth century." He shook his head affirmatively.

"Would that be the case of Veneto?"

"This, _signore_, I'm afraid is a query for the Church Archives in
Venice."

Lorenzo thanked him and strolled out of the building with the
vague but exciting sensation of embarking on a scavenger hunt.

6

LEFKOSIA, *2010*

Marina hit the brakes of her Bossa Nova white Fiat 500 at the university campus and checked the time. She was only a few minutes late for her six-to-nine course, yet that wouldn't deter Professor Papadopoulos, who never made an attempt to conceal his disdain for tardiness, from making a caustic comment at her expense. She rushed up the stairs to A112 only to find it empty. A glimpse at the announcement board confirmed the cancellation of class. Busy with her French clients, Marina didn't have the time to check the university website, but it didn't matter now.

She dragged her fatigued legs to the car. Her French clients had been charming but quite demanding, and balancing their wishes and her study load this last week had not been an effortless task exactly. She still needed to pull herself together and study for next week's final exams - the last ones. She would then need to write her thesis, defend it, get her degree, and finally get a real job – a permanent full-time job. Although multitasking was her middle name, balancing her part-time jobs, guided tours during tourist high season and waiting tables during low season, her studies, and her relationship with George had been more arduous than she had originally anticipated when she proudly declared to her parents that she could make it on her own.

Marina's teenage life had not been easy. Her fifty-eight-year old mother and her sixty-eight-year-old father made an effort to understand their thirteen-year-old daughter's need to blend in with the other girls at school, whose major concern was what to wear at parties. But they never figured that the other girls found it weird that such old folks had a teenage daughter.

The fact that Marina worked weekends and summers to contribute to the family income, especially after her dad's lower limb had been amputated due to diabetes, and that she cared for him in the afternoons when her mother was at work, made it even more difficult to fit in with the other kids at school. Their next-door neighbor's boy, George, would sometimes come round in the afternoons and keep her company when he wasn't playing football with the other boys. As the years went by, their friendship blossomed into romance. *A romance now in sharp decline*, Marina thought, the corners of her mouth twitching.

She made a quick stop at a grocery store. Since she would be home early this evening, she would surprise George with a romantic candle dinner. In all fairness, she thought, she hadn't been very attentive to him lately, but she meant to make it up that night, even though he hadn't been particularly caring either. He would rather spend his free time playing *pilotta[1]* with his friends, or watch football. In the last few months, he even made a habit out of disappearing for the entire weekend on hunting or fishing expeditions. In any event, she was willing to make one more effort to bridge the gap between them – for old times' sake.

She parked the car outside the apartment building on Theseus Street and walked inside. She sighed when she found the elevator out of order again, and with the shopping bags in her hands, she climbed up the seven flights of stairs. Panting, she clutched the shopping bags in one hand while she fished for her house key in her bag.

She got in, kicked the door closed, and placed the shopping bags by the fruit ball on the kitchen counter of their one-bedroom open-plan apartment when she thought she heard voices. Was George home already? She tiptoed into the living room. The voices were coming from the bedroom, although they were not exactly voices. They sounded more like... moans. She pushed the bedroom door open and for a split second, she stood motionless.

"Marina, it's not what it seems," a sweaty, out-of-breath George

---

1 A card game whose origin probably goes back to the Lusignan period.

said while the perplexed girl next to him covered herself up with a pillow. He rested his apologetic olive green eyes on Marina's, smoothed his messy, wavy dark brown hair, and gave her the smile she used to find hard to resist.

All the swear words Marina knew crossed her mind simultaneously like the striking of Zeus' lightning, but he wasn't worth wasting her breath. Without a word, she turned on her heels, picked up her keys and her bag, and dashed to the door.

"Wait! Marina, don't go. I can explain…"

Marina slammed the apartment door behind her. George tried to follow her but tripled over the bed sheet he was covering himself with and fell on all fours. By the time he had managed to get up and to the door, Marina was already out of sight. He cursed, gnashed his teeth, and ran barefoot down the stairs. When he finally got to the street, Marina had already turned the car engine on. George stood enraged and befuddled watching her vanish into the distance. The giggling of two young girls from the sidewalk across the street made him aware of his unusual outfit. He cursed again and went back into the building.

Marina drove aimlessly around Lefkosia, surprised at her own reactions. Yes, she was outraged and disappointed. Yes, her female ego couldn't stomach that she was not enough, but why was her heart not breaking? Did things like these take time until they set it?

She glanced at the setting sun in the distance and put the brooding over her ruined relationship aside for a while. She needed to figure out where she could spend the night. Not that she had that much of a choice. She got on the A1 to Lemesos. Although Marina was a people person, she never really had time for friendships amidst her full-time studies, her part-time jobs, and – what she had believed until then to be – her full-time relationship.

Katerina was the only real friend Marina had. At least, the only one whose door she could knock on – or more precisely, her parents' door. Katerina's parents had always been fond of down-to-earth Marina and considered her a good influence on their up-in-the-clouds daughter. What is more, they felt compelled to try and fill the void of parental support in Marina's life.

Her cell rang for the third continuous time, and Marina turned it off. She had nothing more to say to him - ever. All she needed was a good night's sleep. Then she could decide what she wanted to do with her life.

7

On board Miramare, 1467

In Captain Zanetti's cabin later that evening, father and son were discussing the situation in Cyprus and the developments in the Ottoman-Venetian war over the maritime hegemony of the Aegean and the Adriatic Sea.

"But we can't be losing the war in Albania. Skanderberg has succeeded in lifting the siege of Croia!" Marin cried out.

The captain looked at Marin and nodded. He had always tried to conceal his weakness for his eldest son, who reminded him so much of himself in his youth, and it was more than just the physical resemblance. Despite his artistic and sensitive nature that he inherited from his mother, Marin's drive to learn and achieve – which he got from his father – set him apart from his siblings. Ever since he was a child and Marco Polo was his hero, he loved discussing current affairs with his father who traveled the world.

His beard hadn't started growing yet when the captain put in plain words to him about how Venice's location, diplomacy, and Arsenal had transformed the *Serenissima* into Europe's gateway between the Byzantine Empire and the Islamic civilization. Its location on the Adriatic favored trade with the East, and their skilled diplomatic efforts and intelligence services gave the Venetians an advantage over their European counterparts. Of paramount importance to the *Queen of the Sea* in building its maritime empire, a navy of 3,300 ships, was also the construction of the Arsenal, a complex of state-owned shipyards and armories clustered together - the reason why Venice was capable of standing up to the vast Ottoman Empire for three hundred years and through seven wars.

"News is not good, Marin. As if the plague outbreak amongst the Albanians was not enough, the word is that Skanderberg died of malaria in Lissus. I doubt anyone can replace his influence on the Albanian lords in our favor." The captain got up and stood in front of the porthole. He looked at the rough Sea of *Candia*[1] in the darkness of the moonless, foggy night and straightened his tight waistcoat.

"Surely, you're not worried father. Venice is strong. It's an empire! And not just at sea. She's got eight thousand cavalry enrolled," Marin said with the enthusiastic idealism of youth.

"Empires have fallen before," his father murmured and downed his wine. "Look at the fall of Constantinople. Venice is still joggling trying to reestablish the status quo, but the truth is that the Turks have altered the political map, and we'll have to learn to live with this." He paced up and down, looked over his shoulder, and added, "besides, we are fools!"

Marin furrowed an eyebrow.

"We are cutting down trees for charcoal. Soon, we won't have any trees left to build ships," the captain prophesied.

A knock on the cabin's door put an abrupt end to their conversation.

"Captain! Captain! There's storm coming," a deckhand cried out, and both men dashed to the deck. Storms in the Sea of Candia were never to be taken lightly, especially in the dead of winter.

---

1 Crete.

8

ROVIGO, 2010

Lorenzo called the vice mayor's office, the head of the delegation for the twinning process with the Municipality of Famagusta, for an appointment. Because of a cancellation, the vice mayor could receive him already that same afternoon, a polite female voice informed him, and Lorenzo wondered if that was a good omen.

"Aha... *signor* Zanetti from Ca' Lorenzo with the luscious *cappellacci di zucca!*" The silver-haired politician with a matching moustache walked to the door and shook hands with him.

Lorenzo was happily surprised he remembered him.

"What can I do for you?" asked the vice mayor.

Elaborating on his search proved to be less daunting than Lorenzo had originally feared. A friendly and supportive figure, the vice mayor got on the phone and first called his assistant in and then spoke with the Honorary Consul of Italy in Cyprus, a personal friend of his, requesting all possible assistance in Lorenzo's search.

"Consul Mantovani is Cypriot but speaks fluent Italian."

"Mantovani... That sounds like a name from our region," Lorenzo observed.

"Indeed. Mr. Mantovani's ancestors were of Venetian origin. In fact, he has been able to trace them as far back as 1634 when they first moved to Cyprus. Who knows? You might as well."

The vice mayor gave Lorenzo a list of more contacts, more personal friends of his, who might be of some assistance. He told Lorenzo to feel free to use his name as a reference.

When Raffaella, his assistant, joined them in the office, the vice mayor made the introductions and asked her to assist Mr. Zanetti with his request. He then turned to his guest.

"Well, Lorenzo, I wish you the best of luck with your quest." He shook his hand firmly and offered a sincere smile. Lorenzo thanked him, invited him and his family for dinner, and followed Raffaella to her office where she carefully heard his briefing on his search efforts at the *ufficio anagrafe*[1] and promised to help him with the archives of the *provincia*.

"Before you put your hopes up too high, *signor* Zanetti..."

"Please, call me Lorenzo," he said smoothly.

"Fine... Lorenzo...," she said, tilting her head to the side and fluttering her eyelashes. "I should warn you that you'd be lucky to come across the information you are looking for on property acquisition during this time period. Records dating so far back are hardly ever consistent. You will need to be patient. This can be a time consuming process," Raffaella said and offered him an encouraging smile.

---

1 Registry office.

9

LEMESOS, 2010

Katerina's sympathetic parents invited Marina to stay with them for as long as necessary, but she didn't want to take advantage of their hospitality. In her wakeful night, Marina decided she needed a change here and now. The next morning, she got a new cell phone number that she gave only to her mother and Katerina and made them both swear not to give it to George. She then drove back to Lefkosia while George was at work, sneaked into the apartment, and packed her things. On her way out, she dropped her keys into the letterbox.

Marina was not just moving out of the apartment; she was moving out of his life and away from Lefkosia. Equipped with *Chrysses Aggelies*, a local search and find newspaper, she made several appointments to see apartments for rent while driving back to Lemesos.

She was lucky it only took her a few days to find a small studio in the attic of a building, which once boasted of being a mansion at the beginning of the previous century, on St. Andrews Street, one of Lemesos oldest streets and an integral part of the city's history. In no time, Marina was thrilled to live within walking distance from the seafront promenade on this busy, narrow, jostling street with its quaint buildings and overhanging terraces, under which a cornucopia of small shops, galleries, cafés, restaurants, and bars, vie for attention.

10

EPISKOPI, 1467

It had been almost four weeks since they left the lagoon for the open sea. Marin was standing on deck, leaning on the balustrade, and watching the few docked fishing boats and the small village market come into full view, as the sweaty oarsmen gradually brought the galley into Episkopi Bay. There was excitement among the crew, as Captain Zanetti dexterously navigated the galley to a berth.

If it had been any other voyage, Marin would have ridden to Limassol with the other crew members to trade products, watch a wrestling fight, or seek out a juggler's performance. A typical outing to Limassol would include a decent meal at one of the harbor's taverns by the castle, a few drinks, dancing with a local beauty, and whatever else chance might bring his way - but not this time.

When all the checks were carried out, the captain assigned guard duty to deter the threat of a pirate assault, although this was more of a precautionary measure. Pirates preferred the busy port of Limassol where looting brought them substantially more riches. Father and son disembarked as soon as Marin's trunk was loaded onto the horse-drawn carriage that was awaiting them, courtesy of Andrea Cornaro. Marin set foot on land and took a deep breath of the cold, moist winter air. *This is it*, he thought. *It's happening!*

The captain gave his first officer some last minute instructions, and they set off for the Cornaro sugar mill without delay. They passed by a priest entering a humble Byzantine church with the typical dome, at the small village market, where servants were buying fresh produce at the few stalls. They rode through the vast sugar cane plantations where weather-beaten *paroikoi* and *perperiarii* were cutting the sugar cane and loading it onto horse-drawn carriages to be carried to the mill. Although sugar cane is best harvested in the dry season, the demand for it dictated the lengthening of the harvesting period.

His father had explained to him, how in the feudal system introduced by the Franks, Cypriots were divided into three major classes, the *paroikoi*, or the serfs, the *perperiarii*, who were still bound to the land like the serfs, but who had bought their limited freedom paying fifteen hyperpyra to their master, and the *lefteroi*, or the free citizens, who bought their freedom or were set free by some kind of favor. In the new Frankish regime, there was no place for the *archontes*, the local Greek landowning aristocracy, although, over time, some of them managed to obtain royal privileges and a place in the court of the nobles. Some middle-class Greek town-dwellers were even recruited into the royal administration, thus raising their social and financial status, but these were just a few.

"Look around, Marin. As far as the eye can see and beyond, all this land belongs to the Cornaro," his father explained. He had told him so before, but Marin's brain was only now beginning to grasp the enormity of the responsibility he was entrusted with.

When they finally arrived at the mill, Marin looked at the stone-built structure on the western banks of the Kouris River and then across the river at their rivals at Colossi castle. Although the Order of the Knights of St. John of Jerusalem[1], better known as Hospitallers, had moved their headquarters to Rhodes[2], they maintained their military presence at Colossi castle as well as their profitable sugar mill production.

Jacomo, the lanky, albino mill foreman with the ratty white-blonde beard, greeted them at the entrance and showed them into Andrea Cornaro's office. He ordered a serf, a girl who

---

1 They sought refuge in Cyprus after the capture of Acre in 1291.

2 When they found themselves enmeshed in the politics of the island.

couldn't have been more than eight or nine, to prepare some sage tea for the guests while he sought out Andrea.

The albino first looked in the stoke room, where the fires for the cauldrons in the boiling hall above were lit, but there was no sign of Andrea. He walked out of the premises, for there was no direct access to the other rooms. The boiling hall was partially over the stoke room, as a means to ensure the soot was separated from the sugar. He walked up the external stairway that led to the boiling hall where he found Andrea leaning against the limestone wall, inspecting the work carried out and wearing a pensive face with his arms folded in front of his chest.

"Captain Alexandro Zanetti and his son are here to see you, Sir." Jacomo raised his voice above the factory noise to apprise him of the captain's visit.

Andrea cast his gaze on a ragged serf who drained the sweat from his forehead with his frayed sleeve and ran his filthy fingers through his sticky hair before filling the huge copper cauldron with chopped and crushed sugar cane for the cane juice to be boiled and refined.

"Uh, yes! Thank you, Jacomo," Andrea said and walked briskly to his office, passing by the animal driven mill and the workshop. He cast a quick glance at the small army of serfs who were filling funnel-shaped clay sugar molds and molasses pots to be placed on top of other vessels. In this way, the syrup was separated and flowed through the holes in the bottom, so that crystalline sugar would be formed to a loaf and could be removed from the molds. Andrea marched by a throng of female serfs who freed the dried out sugar from its casing to be sold in the shape of a hat.

A couple of minutes later, Andrea joined them in his office, a spacious room filled with shelves packed with mill records that had accumulated over the years. Andrea hadn't been there for months, but a quick review of the latest ledger entries had left him discontented. Despite Jacomo's efforts, the production seemed to have been unable to match the increasing demand.

"Alexandro!" the man with the auburn hair, the vigilant grey-green eyes, and the thick eyebrows exclaimed and embraced the captain.

"*Consigliere*, it's good to see you again. I trust you are well," the captain said respectfully. "This is my son Marin," he introduced him with pride in his voice. Marin bowed his head briefly and extended his arm, but Andrea embraced him, instead.

"Welcome to Cyprus, your new home. I hope you'll like it here." Andrea scrutinized the young man's expression, but the latter didn't flinch. *Does he have what it takes*, he wondered? Andrea made a mental note of the flash in the young man's alert eyes and the vigor in his movement.

"I'm looking forward to that, uncle," Marin replied assertively.

Andrea invited them both to have a seat. "I hope your journey was not rough," he said when he took a seat behind his heavy oak desk embellished with carved Greco-Roman designs. Marin thought he recognized the athletic figure of Hermes, or Mercury, the patron of commerce.

"Nothing worth mentioning," Alexandro replied, although it had taken everyone's skills on board to sail through the prodigious storm they ran into. "I hope business has been good as usual," the captain, a man of few words, skillfully cut to the chase.

Andrea's bushy eyebrows rose and went down again. "On the whole, yes. We have managed to include most of the royal courts in our clientele. Even common people are now turning to sugar which is neither as rare nor as expensive as honey. The demand has, therefore, grown, but we haven't been able to raise productivity at the same pace yet. We even bought more slaves to boost the output, but that hasn't brought the expected outcome. Meanwhile, competition in Western Europe has been noticeably on the rise with sugar mills mushrooming. Thanks to advisers from Sicily and capital from Genoa, they have managed to break our monopolies."

Andrea paused wistfully and rubbed his right sideburn with his forefinger. "We might even need to reevaluate our options... look into new ventures. And with Giovanni dead, there's no firm hand to supervise the estates... Now, Marin," he turned and faced the young man, "your father must have briefed you on the political state of affairs here in Cyprus."

"I understand that the king might feel vulnerable," Marin said, measuring his words.

"Indeed. James is striving to keep the Turks off his shores. At the same time, Charlotte is exerting herself to gain support from wherever she can in order to get the throne back. Even though the Pope has declined to take any action, the threat of a coalition among the Savoyards, the Genoese, and the Milanese is very real. Not to mention the Florentines or the Catalans," Andrea continued his monolog.

Marin made quick mental associations. Charlotte's husband was the duke of Savoy. The Genoese had a score to settle after they lost Famagusta to the new king, and the Milanese, the Florentines, and the Catalans wanted to see their strong financial interests on the island secured. A bit like a chess game, he thought, where you need to predict the opponent's moves.

"The king is also seeking alliance through marriage, and I need to... assist him in his choice," Andrea said meaningfully. "And here, my dear boy, is where you come into play. I simply cannot be in two places at the same time. I need someone I can trust to run this business and look after the estates for me. Someone with his eyes and ears open for potential profitable ventures while I'm away in Nicosia and while Marco is away in Venice."

Marin was listening to Andrea Cornaro with the deepest veneration, thankful for this exhilarating new life that lay before him. "Show me how I can run this business and I'll have my eyes and ears open day and night. I won't fail you, uncle," he said keenly. Not so many twenty-one-year-olds of ignoble birth gained so much status in one day.

Andrea shook his head and smiled. "All in good time, lad. First, you should rest, and then Jacomo, the foreman, will assist you with anything you need. We must safeguard the secret of sugar production at all costs, so there's nothing I can give you in writing. You need to learn every single detail through observing and memorizing."

"That's fine. I've a good memory," Marin assured him.

Andrea turned to his cousin and asked, "When are you sailing, captain?"

"As soon as we load the cargo and the supplies and my men get a day's rest," the captain replied.

"Excellent. Then we shall dine together tonight."

II

ROVIGO, 2010

Lorenzo's delving into the census, land registry and probate records over the next couple of months shed little, if any, light on his quest. He came across two references in the court archives to a Maria Zanetti, who was prosecuted for gossiping in 1462 and of scolding her husband, Maffeo, in 1463. A reference of greater significance was one recorded in the land registry. It concerned a property acquisition by a certain Alexandro Zanetti in 1469. An extensive search showed that this vast plot of land was divided into shares over the centuries, and Lorenzo's family house formed a tiny fraction of it. The name Marin Zanetti, however, was not mentioned anywhere.

Nonetheless, Lorenzo was determined not to give up. He hadn't exactly become obsessed with this hunt, but it gave him a sense of purpose. What is more, he enjoyed his afternoon chats with Raffaella when her work was done, and they would grab a coffee and discuss his search, usually at one of Rovigo's agritourism farms that Paola enjoyed so much.

Raffaella's assistance was invaluable. She knew the right people in the right places. When on one of those days out she suggested calling *Don* Giuseppe, a childhood friend of her father's, at the Diocese in Venice, Lorenzo was not the least surprised. Raffaella recommended that he take the time and drive to Venice to meet the *padre* in person. That would help speed up the process.

Lorenzo had never been a particularly religious man, but the serenity and the energy he felt when he finally visited *Don* Giuseppe reminded him of how he had once stood in awe while in St. Peter's Basilica in the Vatican. The only ornaments in the *padre's* modest office were an icon of the Madonna and the Pope's photo on the wall. The *padre* walked with slow, yet confident steps to the door to welcome him. Lorenzo looked at the tall ascetic figure with the kind eyes.

"So, you are *signor* Zanetti of Ca' Lorenzo! You probably don't know this, but I've already been to your restaurant once with my dear friend Pietro, Raffaella's father. Our *caparossoli in cassopipa* were delicious!" He beckoned for Lorenzo to take a seat.

"Thank you, *padre*." Lorenzo smiled politely and had a seat. "And thank you for seeing me at such short notice."

"I try to make requests from my home town a priority if circumstances allow. And it just so happens that I am not as busy as usual these days... Can I offer you something to drink?" he asked while taking a seat behind his desk.

"No, thank you. I didn't know you were from Rovigo," Lorenzo said with interest.

"I was born there and went to *scuola elementare* together with Pietro. We practically grew up together until my family moved away," the *padre* said with a touch of nostalgia in his voice. "But enough about me. I understand you are looking for an ancestor of yours."

"Yes, I am."

Lorenzo told him all he knew about the family legend, and *Don* Giuseppe jotted down the details.

"I was wondering what the procedure is so as to gain access to the church archives of the time," Lorenzo finally said.

"You would first of all need to put your request in writing, but that doesn't mean that you would, indeed, be allowed access. Usually, only members of the clergy can access the archives. You understand that this could be a rather time-consuming procedure and that you will have to be patient."

"I suppose there are several people with such a request."

"There are a few," the *padre* replied vaguely.

"In your experience, how long does it usually take?" Lorenzo enquired.

"It's really hard to tell. It depends. My guess would be anything between two to six months."

"Well, thank you for seeing me," Lorenzo said, rising from his seat. "I will put my request in writing right away." He looked at the *padre* rather disappointed.

"Uh! The young! Always impatient," the *padre* said with a smile. "*Signor* Zanetti, you asked me what the procedure is, and I described it to you. I did not say there was no way to help you."

Lorenzo turned and faced him with renewed interest.

"I could perhaps assist the search when my duties are done after prayer." The *padre* smiled serenely at him.

"Thank you, *padre*. Thank you so much."

"There's nothing to thank me for, child. My secretary will guide you through the process. We will need your birth certificate to create your genealogical tree. Leave your contact details with my secretary before you leave. I will personally get in touch when the search is complete. Godspeed!"

12

LEMESOS, *2010*

Marina spent the next couple of months adjusting to her new life without George in her new studio in a new city. Deep down, she knew they had stayed in this relationship reluctant to admit their love had faded away. Even if out of gratitude for the friendship he had offered her when she most needed it, Marina would never have initiated a break up with him, but catching him cheating unmasked everything. In a way, it was a relief.

While most other students were having fun at the beach during the day and clubbing at night, Marina worked hard and saved money for the fall semester. In her free time, she tried to make the most out of her sixteen square meters of living space. She painted the walls in her favorite colors – soft, warm maize yellow and cheerful peach orange. She purchased a lace curtain for the only window of her studio, and with sheer determination, she assembled the DIY furniture she bought. She filled the only free corner with an olive tree and the shelves with her books and put up a poster of Venice on the wall – her dream destination. When everything was in place, she invited Katerina and her boyfriend Andy over for dinner to celebrate.

As the days went by, she realized that Katerina was doing a great job keeping George away from her, but her own mother was beginning to soften. At first, the elderly woman was furious with her son-in-law-to-be's behavior. But as the days turned into weeks, with his constant pleading to at least be able to talk to her and say how sorry he was, the seeds of doubt began to blossom.

13

1467

Like a sponge, Marin absorbed every little detail about the work at the sugar mill in the next few months. He found out that the mill relied on the waterwheel and its grinding systems. In addition to the animal-driven grinding wheel and millstone, at the Cornaro mill, they also applied a more technologically advanced multi-floor, gear-based, horizontal waterwheel crushing and grinding system.

One of the largest problems when refining sugar, from a quality standpoint, was how to handle the soot, the ash, and the other byproducts from the fire necessary for the boiling process. In the Cornaro mill, they addressed this question by separating the facilities into four main sections, the store room-workshop, the mill area, the boiling hall and the stoke rooms. Another novelty at the Cornaro mill was the copper[1] cauldrons. Copper cannot only be hammered flat with little effort, but it also naturally reacts with sugar and prevents it from recrystallizing.

Marin quickly understood that the production of sugar depended on three major factors, slaves and serfs - as it was extremely labor intensive - water, and wood. Acquiring slaves partly resolved the issue of hands needed. The workforce at the mill now surpassed four hundred, not to count the several other hundreds of serfs who worked the fields.

As sugar cane has a long growing season, it requires a substantial amount of water. The Kouris River, with its elaborate aqueduct system, transported the water needed to irrigate the fields and power the grinding millstones as well as to clean and care for equipment. What Marin soon realized was that in the dry season, especially after periods of drought, Kouris wouldn't flow

---

1 Copper was profuse on the island. Cyprus, 'Kypros' in Greek, may have given the metal its Latin name, *cuprum*.

swiftly enough to provide adequate power, and that slowed down the process. He made a mental note to discuss this with Andrea at their next meeting. There had to be a way to improve the water power efficiency. Perhaps they should seek an engineer's advice. At least, recurring conflict between the Cornaro and the Hospitallers over the legal rights to use the water of the river had abated during the rainy season.

Firewood seemed to be the major cause of delay in production. The lumberjacks had to cut down trees farther and farther away from the mill as the surrounding area had been gradually deforested. They were rapidly reaching the boundaries of the Cornaro estate. Marin would have to figure out a way to secure more timber. Moreover, he realized how cutting corners in the maintenance of machinery caused further holdups, and he gave orders for immediate amendments.

For the most part, the young Venetian took to liking his life in Cyprus at once. Not only was he now the 'master'- he still smiled inwardly at that - but he enjoyed the cultural osmosis that reminded him of home. Fifteenth century Cyprus resembled a mosaic of ethnicities in which various elements fused at the edges as foreigners gradually acquired a Cypriot consciousness and some even spoke Greek. Especially after the Synod of Florence unified the two Christian churches, the intermingling of the Greek and Latin population in Cyprus altered the Frankish society on the island. This was a time when Latin priests would switch churches so as to be able to marry and Latin laymen so as to divorce. Even some Latin aristocracy had switched church so as to gain the favor of Queen Elena.

It didn't take long for Marin to comprehend that there were two distinct societies on the island, one foreign - the royalty and the nobility, which was made up of various communities, 'states within the state' almost - and one native. The majority of the local population was Greek-speaking Orthodox peasants, farmers, or craftsmen. Among them, there were thousands of

Armenians, Maronites[2], and Hebrews. Cyprus gave shelter to the influx of refugees as Crusaders retreated, losing one territory after another and when Constantinople fell to the Ottoman Turks in 1453.

In order to consolidate their power over the Greek population, the Lusignan Dynasty had offered fiefs and other grants to European knights who came in search of social advancement, profit, and adventure in a newly established kingdom. The experience of the Knights Templar taught the Lusignans a valuable lesson. If Cyprus was to be held long, a small garrison would not suffice to control the people. A large number of men with a vested interest in preserving the new regime were needed.

---

2 The Maronites belong to the Eastern Christian cult of the Catholic Church which is based in Antioch and were named after Saint Maron (350-410 AD) who lived in the region of Apamea in Syria. Maronites came to Cyprus in four major migrations between the 8th and the 13th century AD.

14

ROVIGO, *2010*

Lorenzo lifted the collar of his black blazer and kneeled by his wife's gravestone. Paola did the same and silent tears rolled down her soft cheeks. She put a bouquet of white orchids, Beth's favorite flowers, in a vase.

It had been exactly one year without her, but there were still moments when Lorenzo was expecting to see her light figure walk through the door. "I miss you, Beth,' he said, bringing the fingers of his right hand to his lips and then lowering them onto her gravestone.

"Daddy, do you really think that mommy can see us from heaven?"

"I'm sure she sees what a wonderful young lady you have turned into, and she's very proud of you." Lorenzo offered his daughter a congenial smile.

"Maybe not so wonderful," the sad-faced girl replied.

"What makes you say that?"

"Daddy... I'm afraid I don't remember her. I know what she looks like in photos, but I don't remember her face." Paola sighed and fixed her gaze on the gravestone as if all the answers she was looking for could be found there.

Lorenzo put his own devastating feelings aside and cleared the lump in his throat. "Come here," he said as he opened his arms for her to hide in.

"You don't have to remember her face. You just need to remember that mommy loved you more than anything in the whole wide world and that she's always looking down on earth smiling at you. So, whenever you need her, just look at the sky and smile back."

Lorenzo watched Paola lift her head up and look at the sky. Her lips formed a smile – a timid one at first, and then a wide one. When she was calm again, they rose to their feet, and Lorenzo cleared the moisture off the knees of his black jeans as best as he could. He held her little hand in his, as they walked to the classic red Alfa Romeo Duetto Spider. He helped his lost-in-her-thoughts daughter with the child car seat and then sat behind the wheel without turning the engine on. It began to drizzle again. He focused his gaze on Beth's grave, contemplating all the plans they had made together until the trembling cell phone in his pocket brought him back to reality.

"*Signor* Zanetti, this is *Don* Giuseppe," the familiar, gentle voice said.

"Good morning, *padre*. Any news?" Lorenzo asked in tense anticipation. He hadn't heard from him for months. As all other leads rendered no meaningful result, he had almost given up on Marin.

"Yes, but let me remind you that records dating so far back are not consistent," the *padre* said stoically. "I have been able to trace two men by the name of Marin Zanetti in the time period you are interested in who might be related to your genealogical tree. One of them was born in 1445, *fu de fornaio*[1] Maffeo Zanetti. The other one was born in 1446, the son of Alexandro Zanetti, *capitano delle galere al viazzio del traffico*[2]"

"What was the father's name again?" Lorenzo's mind was racing. Could there be a link to Alexandro Zanetti with the land acquisition in 1469?

"Alexandro," the *padre* repeated, and Lorenzo felt his adrenaline spiking.

"Well, the first one seems to have married here and become the father of three sons and four daughters who never left Veneto, for they married and had children here, except for two who died of the plague."

---

1 The baker's son.

2 Captain of trade galley.

"What about the captain's son?" Lorenzo tried not to sound impatient.

"Well, there is less information about him. In fact, there is no reference to him after his baptism… no wedding, no death registered. He might have moved away at a young age. It must have been easy for him, considering his father's profession," the *padre* deduced.

"Is it possible he might have returned to Italy but not to Veneto?"

"It's possible, but our records wouldn't hold such information."

"I don't know how I can begin to thank you, *padre*." Lorenzo brought his hand to his forehead sensing Marin calling him.

"There is nothing to thank me for, child. I am glad I could be of service. My secretary will be faxing you the relevant documents later today. May you find all the answers you are looking for. Godspeed!"

Lorenzo held on to his cell phone and tried to take on board all this information. It was as if everything was pointing at the direction of furthering his search in Cyprus.

"Who was that, daddy?"

Lorenzo's eyebrows lifted up and went down again. "That… That was *Don* Giuseppe. He's been helping me trace an ancestor."

"A what?"

"An ancestor. Like a great-great-great grandfather."

"And? Did you trace him?"

"I might have. It seems he lived on Cyprus, an island. I might want to go there one day and see if I can find out more about him."

"Okay." To Paola, her father's plan obviously didn't sound complicated at all.

15

Lemesos, *2010*

Marina was working on her thesis when the sound of her ring tone interrupted her thoughts. She checked the screen. It was her mother.

"Marina, George was here again asking about your address. I can't do this anymore. You need to deal with this, or I'll give him your new cell phone number. I've had enough." Her mother only stopped to catch her breath. "You were so crazy about him you even ran away with him. Now, you won't even talk to him. I don't understand you young people. In my time, you would have got married from the beginning. End of story!"

Marina took a deep breath. Her mother did have a point. This was her problem, not her mother's. George knew exactly which strings to pull to get her to talk to him.

"I believe that even in your generation the notion of a divorce was not so uncommon, unless, of course, women didn't mind sharing their husbands with the other women in the village."

"Men in my generation did no such things," her mother retorted.

You wish, Marina thought, but instead she said, "Well, men in my generation do, and I have no intention to live with it. I understand George can be very persuasive when he wants to. I bet you already feel sorry for him and consider me cruel. Anyway, I'll talk to him. Just don't give him my number. Please!"

Marina knew when George put an idea in his head, he could be unrelenting. Although she had neither time nor energy in excess to deal with him at the moment, she couldn't hide behind her mother like that. Unfalteringly, she grabbed her keys, walked to the nearest public telephone, and dialed his number.

"Hello." His voice brought back memories of a decade.

"Hi."

"Marina?" George couldn't believe his ears.

"You wanted to talk to me?"

"What are you doing in Lemesos?"

Of course, he could see the number on his screen.

"George, just tell me what you want. And leave my mom alone. She's a lonely, old woman. She doesn't deserve this harassment."

"Yeah, she told me about your dad. I'm sorry. I would have come to the funeral if I had known. And I'm sorry about bothering your mom. I didn't know how else I could find you."

Marina sighed. "What do you want, George?" she asked quietly.

"Things to be the way they used to be. I love you."

"You have a funny way of showing that."

The image of him sweating over that girl in her own bed made her stomach turn, but that was not why she was calling. He had to understand it was over and leave her mother alone.

"It was a mistake. Just once. I'm sorry. It won't happen again, I promise," he pleaded.

"You know, this is not just about the girl. Let's be honest here. We both knew things between us hadn't been the way they used to be in a long, long time."

"How can you throw away all these years we've had together?"

Marina refused to feel guilty about it and was proud she managed to keep a steady voice. "If my memory serves me right, *you* are the one who did."

"I don't want to lose you, Marina!"

"It's time you moved on, George. I have," she said gently but firmly. "Goodbye, George," she said and hung up when he remained perplexed and silent.

Exhausted, she dragged her feet to the pier, sat on a bench, and fixed her gaze on the horizon. Ever since she was a little girl in Kato Pyrgos, the beach was her sanctuary. This is probably why she felt more at home in Lemesos than she did in Lefkosia.

16

1467

Notwithstanding his duties at the palace and masterful endeavors to sway the king's decision in favor of a Venetian bride, Andrea undertook Marin's tutoring in the state of affairs in Cyprus and the Cornaro enterprises personally. Upon returning from the capital late one evening, Andrea was pleased to see Marin wasn't wasting his time playing *pilotta* or, worse, getting drunk, two fashionable forms of entertainment among the young – and the not so young. Instead, Marin was industriously going over the sugar mill books he had brought to the estate to burn the midnight oil. The older man smiled privately at the young man's determination not to fail him.

Andrea Cornaro, a very well-educated, perspicacious merchant with the Midas touch, rose to nobility by identifying - even creating – opportunities. He was a man who inspired respect even among his adversaries. This respect motivated his people to work hard to surpass his expectations of them.

"Good evening, uncle," Marin said darting to his feet. "We were not expecting you tonight. Everyone's gone to bed. I'll get you some supper."

"It's all right, Marin. I've already eaten. But let's have some commandaria[1], shall we?"

Andrea took a seat in his favorite armchair covered in vermilion cordovan, studded with nails and bordered with fringes. It

---

1 A sweet desert wine with the oldest appellation for a wine in the world. In antiquity, commandaria was a popular drink at festivals worshiping Aphrodite, Cyprus' patron deity. Legend has it that the King of England, Richard Coeur-de-Lion, enjoyed it so much that he pronounced it 'the wine of kings and the king of wines'. In the early thirteenth century, at the first ever wine tasting competition, *La Bataille des Vins*, or the Battle of Wines, which included wines from all over Europe, the winner was a wine from Cyprus widely believed to be Commandaria.

almost resembled a throne with its carved gilded canopies. The two hound dogs sat at each side of the armchair. Andrea placed the cushion of cloth of gold behind his neck and patted their heads.

Marin added some firewood to the fireplace with the monumentally sculpted chimney, which depicted the Lion of San Marco, and took a blue glass bottle decorated with cold gold and enamel technique and two glasses from the *dressoir*. He poured some *commandaria*, and offered his uncle a glass.

"*Conte* Visconti's wife has died, while giving birth, I think. Anyway, the funeral is tomorrow, and I'd like you to come with me."

"Of course," Marin replied. "Uh... Who's *Conte* Visconti?"

"The *conte* is a powerful man and a shrewd businessman. He has augmented his inherited family fortune by acquiring the leasing rights for the Limassol salt lake from Ioannis Podocatoro. The salt lake was Podocatoro's reward for his services to King Janus... A very profitable venture, indeed," he added almost talking to himself. He paused for a moment and then asked, "Everything running smoothly at the mill and the estates?"

"Yes, everything's fine." Marin hesitated for a moment. "I believe we need to find a way to strengthen the water power."

"Are the Hospitallers causing trouble again?" Andrea asked quietly. A cool-headed man, he liked to study all the facts at hand carefully before reaching conclusions.

"No, no. It's just that I've noticed that when the river doesn't flow swiftly, we don't have sufficient power for the waterwheel. If we could bring an engineer to see the mill..."

"We're lucky. Guglielmo Fontana is here to make suggestions for the fortification of the Nicosia walls. Perhaps he could take a day and visit the mill."

Marin cleared his throat before he said, "Uncle, you know that we've exhausted a lot of the timber on the estate."

Andrea met the young man's ambitious gaze and said encouragingly, "And?"

"And... I've been thinking that we could use the deforested land to cultivate cotton. It is my understanding that Venice is having a hard time putting up with the constant increase in demand in the fustian industry in South Germany and Switzerland. All the important centers, Biberach, Augsburg, Constance, and Ulm procure their raw material from Venice. It's an industry with an annual turnover of a quarter of a million ducats! And of no lesser importance, cultivating cotton is far less labor intensive than producing sugar." Marin held his breath until his uncle finally spoke.

"Cotton! Hmm..." Andrea smiled approvingly. "By our next meeting, I'd like you to give me a full account regarding the investment cost entailed in the startup and maintenance of such an enterprise, as well as the profit you expect it to yield." He sniffed the complex and passionate aroma of his golden-ruby colored *commandaria* and savored the everlasting aftertaste. He stretched his legs on the Aragon leather carpet and closed his tired eyes for a moment.

17

ROVIGO, 2010

With his research concluded in Italy, Lorenzo invited Raffaella to dinner to thank her for all her support in facilitating his search. It was the least he could do. Lorenzo checked the time and then the entrance, expecting to see the familiar figure walk through the door, but Raffaella was running unusually late that night.

Lorenzo cast his gaze at the prolific use of wood that gave his restaurant a warm, cozy touch. He shifted his gaze from the marble fireplace, framed by an amber glow, to the rich deep red curtains, the reproductions of Renaissance masterpieces of Italian art, and the discreet backlighting that added a touch of amicable elegance to the ambience, and a self-satisfied grin spread across his face knowing he did a good job decorating the place. He then checked the entrance one more time, totally unprepared for the surprise he was in for that evening.

The woman who showed up at his restaurant had little resemblance to the self-effacing vice-mayor's assistant. The spectacles were gone, her chestnut brown hair, now lightened with blonde highlights, was worn down, and the dark professional suits were substituted by a crimson thigh-length chiffon dress with a deep décolleté. The fine fabric clinched in at the waist and skimmed her body. Lorenzo looked at her from head to toes arching his brows at her metamorphosis.

"Wow, you look beautiful!" he said in all honesty.

"Thank you," Raffaella accepted his compliment tilting her head to the side and fluttering her eyelashes. She had spent the entire afternoon at the beautician, the hairdresser, and at various boutiques looking for the right dress.

Over dinner, Lorenzo kept her up to date with *Don* Giuseppe's findings. If Raffaella had expected a different topic that night, she didn't show it. Slowly, she crossed one leg over the other with her chest puffed out.

"I think it's time I continued the search in Cyprus," Lorenzo said, making an effort not to stare at her inviting large breasts.

"Great! I would love to take a few days off work, too." She daintily ran her middle finger around the rim of her glass, looking deeply into his eyes.

Lorenzo loosened the collar of his shirt with his first finger and glanced uneasily around the restaurant. "Will you please excuse me a minute? I think they need a hand in the kitchen."

They didn't. He needed to walk away. On the brink of stage fright, he realized he still wasn't ready to get romantically involved. Besides, he had to look for Marin, he thought. He didn't have time for that now.

"Don't you look smart tonight!" Antonio, his sous-chef, said when he came into the kitchen. "We're fine here, so why don't you just go and enjoy your dinner? And your friend. She looks hot!"

Lorenzo smiled but refrained from answering. It hadn't been more than a week since he went out on a date again, but Beth's image chaperoned him embarrassingly. Sofia, his sister, had introduced him to Barbara, a friend of hers who had recently moved to Rovigo so as to split the traveling distance between her antique stores in Venice and Ferrara. Sofia had insisted so much on his asking her out to dinner that he finally humored her. Barbara was, by all standards, gorgeous and sophisticated. A successful businesswoman, she was accustomed to taking the lead, but Lorenzo needed more time.

When he got back to the table, he put a friendly smile on his face and treated Raffaella courteously for the rest of the meal. Right after espresso, she excused herself – something about having to get up early the next morning. She thanked him again for a wonderful dinner and left. Lorenzo watched her walk away experiencing an amalgam of relief, flattery, and frustration.

He poured himself another Armagnac and wondered if it was possible that Marin never returned to his homeland. For all he knew, he might have met some beautiful Cypriot girl, married her, had lots of children with her there, and lived happily ever after. Could it be that his name was not erased in the course of time? Mantovani's wasn't.

18

LEFKOSIA, 2010

At the campus cafeteria check-out counter, Marina looked over her shoulder at the sound of Katerina's voice calling out her name and spotted her friend walking swiftly toward her.

"Want a snack, too?" Marina asked before stepping away from the counter, but the girl with the pierced nose and a tattoo of the Chinese word for happiness above her right ankle showed no interest in earthy needs like food. She came to stand and hop close to Marina. Katerina might not have been the brightest student on campus, but she had a heart of gold, a quality Marina appreciated deeply in her friend.

"He did it!" she cried out, obviously on cloud nine.

Marina shook her head to slow her down. "*Who* did *what?*"

Marina carried her tray to an empty table by the window overlooking the clock tower square filled with students and professors rushing to and from class. Katerina followed her playing with the flock of cherry red on her short iron-flat black hair.

"Andy. He popped the question! Last night. Look!" She stretched her hand in front of Marina's nose showing off her engagement ring.

Marina put the tray down and gave her friend a squeezing hug. "Congratulations! I'm so happy for you guys."

"Thanks, Marina *mou*[1]"

"Well, this calls for celebration," Marina said decisively.

"Tonight. Just you, Marios, Andy, and me. I want you to be my maid of honor and Marios is going to be the best man."

---

[1] A form of endearment.

"Great. What do I bring?"

"You don't bring anything. Andy and Marios are taking care of everything... Have I mentioned Marios is single?" Katerina looked at her friend sideways.

"And I care because?" Marina asked, raising an eyebrow. Since George's infidelity, Katerina had been trying to set her up on a date.

"Oh, he's only one of the hottest guys on campus, drives a brand new Mercedes, and he's going to take over his dad's company one day," Katerina said, stretching her hand in front of her admiring her engagement ring.

"If your description is accurate, he won't stay single for long. Have you told your parents yet?" Marina casually changed the subject.

"No. I'll tell them this afternoon. Oh, I almost forgot. I ran into George this morning." She grimaced.

"Where?" Marina asked alarmed.

Katerina lowered her conspiratorial voice. "Here, on campus. He's still looking for you."

"Don't I know that?" Marina's question sounded more like a statement.

She contemplated telling her friend about talking to George on the phone, but that was not the right moment, she decided. Katerina deserved to enjoy her happiness to the fullest.

"What did you tell him?"

"The usual story. We have lost contact since we're no longer taking any courses together - you writing your thesis from home and all. I didn't fail to remind him what a prick he is and that he was history the moment he cheated on you and that he should best forget all about you because last time I checked, you were dating some gorgeous, rich guy - someone like Marios." Katerina looked at her friend meaningfully.

"Thanks, Katerina *mou*." Marina didn't dignify the implied question with a response.

"Marina, you need someone to protect you, someone like Marios," Katerina insisted.

"I can manage on my own. Thanks for the vote of confidence," Marina said, shaking her head dismissively.

Katerina glanced at her watch. "Oh, I'm late for class again! I have to run. I'll see you tonight."

19

1467

"So, tell me, uncle, the news from the palace." Marin helped himself to some *soutzoukos*[1] from the silver tray close to him.

"The king is still considering his options for marriage and alliances." Andrea swirled the *commandaria* to let in the aromatic finesse and complexity of the *Xynisteri*[2] and *Mavro*[3] combination.

"Do you think he will make up his mind soon?"

It was more than evident that the king needed to have his back covered.

"Success in politics depends upon securing the right alliances and making the right moves at the right time. Everything flows; nothing stands still... Right now, things don't look all that favorable for the king." The tired man rubbed his neck for comfort.

"Is this because of the economic stagnation and the social and political uncertainties?"

"What do you know about that?" Andrea looked at Marin wearing an inscrutable face.

"Only what I hear. That the government is tiptoeing around foreign merchants because a change of trading routes through Alexandria would mean fewer tariffs and charges. To make things worse, the successive Black Death epidemics have led to a fall in demand for foreign products in Europe and labor shortages here. We know that first hand at the mill and the estates... From what I hear, the drought and the locusts are likely to cause another harvesting failure this year. The Turks are lurking around the corner, and Charlotte's supporters are not happy

---

1 A string of almonds dipped in thickened grape juice.

2 An ancient indigenous grape variety.

3 An ancient indigenous grape variety.

to be deprived of certain prerogatives. And they are critical of the king's amorous escapades. Is he really as handsome and as strong as people say?"

"I see you have your ears open." The severe expression on Andrea's face made the young man's smirk grow faint.

"And your assumptions are right." Pensively, Andrea swirled the *commandaria* in his glass again before he took another sip. In a lighter vein, he added, "I invited the king to a feast after hunting last week. He took his time admiring Caterina's portrait."

"Caterina who?" Marin wondered out loud raising an eyebrow.

"My niece, Marco's daughter." Andrea's eyes focused on the glass in his hand.

"I didn't realize you have her portrait." As hard as Marin squeezed his brain, he couldn't recall any such portrait.

"Not when you last visited. It's new. I have only recently received it from Venice." Andrea met the young man's stare.

"You're trying to induce the king to ask her hand in marriage!" Marin said struck by epiphany.

"There's nothing wrong with testing the waters. His comments on her gentle beauty were, indeed, encouraging." Andrea's eyelids felt sluggish.

If the king finally decided in favor of a Venetian bride, why not Caterina, he thought? After all, her great-grandfather, John Comnenus, was the Greek emperor of Trebizond. This marriage might have seemed like a power game above the Cornaro league at the time, and Caterina was only thirteen, but still at a legal age for marriage. Besides, such moves were hardly ever made over night.

"That would be a brilliant move!"

"How so?" Andrea asked in his usual dialectical method.

"Well, to begin with, the Republic is mighty enough to protect

Cyprus, which is the king's primary concern. Then, it would be to the _Serenissima's_ benefit to have an outpost so far east. That would ensure its trade routes. And if that were the case, that would be beneficial to us, the Cornaro enterprises I mean, too. After all, it would be fairly short-sighted for the Republic to put all its eggs in the basket of Alexandria and the Muslims."

"Quite right, my boy. Quite right," Andrea said, considering that Marin's training was almost concluded. That came in handy. Andrea intended to stay by the king's side as much as possible. He was certain he would soon be consenting to the engagement.

A shrewd politician, James II would soon see his perfect ally in the face of the Republic of San Marco. The marriage would seal the long-lasting alliance. Marco was already preparing the ground in Venice. With his daughter's potential engagement, the family's good name would not only be restored but their status elevated and cemented. The Council of Ten, however, was not willing to write them a blank check. Before the marriage, Caterina would be declared an adopted daughter of the Venetian Republic. Hence, in future, the Most Serene Republic could inherit the right of succession to the throne and possession of the kingdom itself.

"I wonder how wise it is for the king to prefer the house of Cornaro so openly," Andrea said, almost talking to himself.

"The Republic should be glad the king chooses a Venetian bride!"

"Our fellow-Venetians' jealousy should be feared," Andrea said, bringing his right forefinger to his auburn sideburn and remained silent for a while.

"What if... What if he doesn't prefer Caterina openly?" Marin suggested.

Andrea looked at his protégé with a glint in his eyes and built upon the young man's idea.

"An ambassador could perhaps be dispatched to Venice seeking alliance with the *Serenissima* and asking from the senate the hand of some high-born maid of Venice in marriage to his highness, the King of Cyprus! Brilliant, Marin," he exclaimed.

"There's only one catch. How can we be sure they will suggest Caterina be his queen?"

"Yes, I see what you mean." Andrea rubbed his chin. "It's feasible," he said after some thought. "The king will need to instruct the ambassador in all secrecy just how and whom to choose."

Marin poured some more *commandaria* and clinked his glass against Andrea's. "To Queen Caterina," Marin proposed with a smile, and the two men drank to that.

"Oh, uncle, I almost forgot. I had a request a few days ago, and I'm not sure how to best handle this case." Marin scratched the back of his head.

"What case?"

"Well, Timotheos, Stephania's father, serfs on the estates, received a visit by the matchmaker from Colossi. It seems that a serf from the Hospitaller estates saw the girl at some local church festival and has asked for her hand in marriage. Timotheos has requested permission for Stephania to marry and go and live in Colossi."

"Oh, no, no." Andrea shook his head negatively with vigor. "You tell Timotheos, if he wants his daughter married to the Colossi lad, the boy needs to come to us. We could always use an extra pair of hands. Not the other way around."

"What if the Hospitallers refuse to let him come and live here?" Marin asked curiously.

"Well, I'm sure there are plenty of young men on our estates who might be interested in the girl," Andrea replied indifferently.

Marin looked at him through narrow eyes but kept his thoughts to himself.

20

ROVIGO, 2010

Lorenzo took the calendar in his hands making a quick mental calculation. He always closed the restaurant for a couple of weeks after the Christmas holidays. This time, he could combine the search for Marin with a brief vacation, and he had never been to Cyprus before. He could take up on Sofia and leave Paola with her. It would be perhaps wiser. January is not the best of times to travel with a child.

He was determined not to let anything lessen his enthusiasm. Not even the fact that a couple of history professors he tried to contact at the University of Cyprus to help in his search had not responded to his emails yet. They were on vacation, he surmised.

He searched the Internet for flight alternatives and travel agencies. Since he didn't want to leave Paola behind for a long time, his trip would be short, but he meant to make the most of it. Lorenzo always allowed himself small luxuries when he was on vacation as compensation for his working hard all year round. This time, he opted for private tours.

A few hours and several emails later, he received a list of an agency's private guides' brief profiles for his kind consideration. The case of a private guide by the name of Marina Zanettou piqued his curiosity. She had only a few years of experience but an attention-grabbing name - the same as his ancestor's.

He wondered what the odds were and decided that she might be as good a starting point for his search as any. He browsed through her profile. She seemed to have a special interest in Cyprus' Frankish and Venetian periods that were important to him. She spoke poor Italian, but that didn't matter, as he was fluent in English.

The email icon flashed on his screen. The travel agency enquired whether he had any particular interests or dietary or other needs. Would it sound bizarre if he wrote that he was looking for an ancestor who died over five hundred years ago, he wondered?

Before leaving the house to pick up Paola, he booked a flight, a room at the Intercontinental, and replied to the travel agency's email requesting Ms Zanettou's services as a private guide, giving the flight details and relevant information.

On the way to Paola's kindergarten, he speed dialed his sister. "Hey, beautiful."

"Hey, handsome. What do you want this time?" Sofia scolded her little brother gently, recognizing the line he used whenever he wanted to ask something of her in a roundabout way.

"Whatever do you mean?" he asked in an ostensibly innocent tone of voice and snorted.

"Out with it!" Sofia said with a half smile.

"Remember the family legend about Marin Zanetti?"

"Yes, and?" Sofia wondered what that had to do with anything.

"I'll try and find out what happened to him," he said and envisaged his sister's face at the sound of it.

"You will what?" Hunting a dead ancestor was the last thing she had expected to hear.

"I'm going to Cyprus to see if I can track him down." Lorenzo snickered.

"Finally! It was about time you took a vacation. You don't need an excuse to get some rest, you know. How long will you be away?" She had told him time and time again he should get some time off work just to relax and to start dating again – with Barbara preferably.

"I'm leaving on Monday, but I'll be back Friday."

"So soon? Why don't you stay longer? And don't you worry about Paola. I'm sure she'll be happy to spend a few days with us and play with Gianfranco all day long... Gianfranco, no more chocolates!"

Lorenzo wondered how his sister always managed to have eyes in the back of her head. She used to do the same with him when they were children. "Thank you, Sofia. I don't know why, but this is something I just have to do. But I don't want to miss my weekends with Paola. Before I know it, she'll be a grown woman. I want to enjoy having her with me as long as it lasts."

"I'm sure that will take a while. And when you are there, try and have some fun for a change. You don't have to spend the entire time hunting a dead man," Sofia suggested with a smile.

"Yes, ma'am. Will do."

"Oh, by the way, Barbara was asking about you the other day," Sofia said cautiously.

"It's not going to work, Sofia. It's too early," he said, loosening the collar of his shirt.

"Lorenzo, a whole year is not early. What's wrong with Barbara anyway? She's beautiful, educated, rich, and very fond of you." There was no doubt in her mind that Barbara was the perfect match.

"I don't know. She's intimidating, I guess," he blurred out the first excuse that crossed his mind.

Sofia bit her lower lip and kept her thoughts to herself. Beth's death and the responsibility for Paola had changed her kid brother. Before they hung up, Lorenzo invited them all for dinner at the restaurant.

Outside Paola's kindergarten a few minutes later, Lorenzo went down on his knees for his hugs and kisses in the hullabaloo of hordes of hasty, little creatures passing them by.

He helped her with her seat, got in, shifted into reverse and checked his daughter's face in the mirror. "How was school?"

"Great! It was Marco's birthday today, and he brought a birthday cake to class."

"Nice... Did you learn something new today?"

He turned right at the Due Torri, the two medieval towers that once formed part of the *castello* which dates back to the eleventh century. Torre Donà, 66m in height, was probably the highest brick tower of its time.

"We learned about farm animals, and next week we're going to visit a farm," Paola announced with her face ablaze with excitement.

"That sounds fun... Uh, Paola, about next week. I thought of going on a trip... Remember my ancestor in Cyprus?" Lorenzo saw her nodding in the mirror. "I'd like to find out what happened to him. You can come with me if you like," he tested her.

"But then I'd miss the farm visit. Can't I just stay with Gianfranco?"

Lorenzo checked his daughter's face in the mirror again. "You're sure about this?"

Paola nodded and sticking her nose to the car window, she asked, "Where are we going? This is not the way home!"

"I thought you might want to have lunch at the Parco Regionale," Lorenzo said and saw the smile on his daughter's face. Parco Regionale Veneto del Delta was one of her favorite places.

21

LEMESOS, *2011*

Marina looked out the campus library window and deliberated over her options, given the bleak state of her finances. The temporary job waiting tables she got during the Christmas holidays helped her stay afloat until now, but help was no longer wanted at the nadir of January's low season that immediately followed the festive days. She counted the money in her wallet. *Pathetic,* she thought! Renting her own studio and having to pay for all the expenses by herself evolved into a Sisyphean task. She sighed.

So far, she had refused to ponder the ramifications of failing to secure a steady income. Now, the possibility of putting her tail between her legs and moving back to her parents' house in the remote village of Kato Pyrgos, a dreadful prospect after having spent six years as an independent adult, was staring her in the face. The mere reflection of returning unemployed to her birthplace left the bitter taste of defeat in her mouth.

When Marina finished school, she went to live in Lefkosia with George. She had first enrolled in the one-year Tourist Guides' School and then in the business administration program at the University of Cyprus while working as a guide, mostly between May and October, an arrangement relatively compatible with her study load. At first, George was drafted in the army for two years and then got a sales job in a telecommunications store. Her parents were unable to understand why the two young people wouldn't marry as the years went by. Marina had a hard time justifying that even to herself. Eventually, it turned out it was for the better.

She glanced at her watch, picked up her bag and the books from the table, checked them out and walked out of the building. It was drizzling. She put her umbrella up and checked her missed calls. She ignored them all but the one from a travel agency she worked for.

"Marina, I know this comes on a short notice, but the request has just come in. We have an Italian client who has requested your private guide services starting coming Monday until Friday. Are you available?"

Although a very kind man, the head of incentives and private tours department never seemed to have time for pleasantries. Marina feared that he had been on the verge of a stroke or a heart attack lately. Then again, that was probably just a repercussion of the international financial crisis and the worldwide plummeting of the tourism industry.

"Sure. Any details?"

"Forwarding his email as we speak. I'll keep you posted," he said and hung up.

"Yes!" Marina exclaimed triumphantly raising her fist it in the air. She ignored Marios's calls but decided to return Katerina's call. "Hey, what's up?"

"Why are you avoiding him?" Katerina cut to the chase in an almost accusing tone of voice.

Marina grinned. "Exactly, whom am I avoiding?" She knew whom she meant. She just liked to irritate Katerina when she became bossy.

"Marios! He's been trying to get in touch with you since the engagement party, but you never return his calls. Why? He's such a good catch!" Katerina never really understood Marina when it came to men.

"Because of that."

"Run this by me one more time!"

"He's a good catch, right? You know it. I know it. He knows it. Pretty much every chick on campus knows it. Katerina, I'm not going to trade one George for another, so you can tell Marios – if he hasn't figured it out already - he's wasting his time waiting for me. Case closed."

Katerina knew it was pointless to argue further. When Marina made up her mind, it was next to impossible to change it.

22

1467

Guglielmo Fontana accepted Andrea Cornaro's invitation to visit the sugar mill in Episkopi. After a careful inspection of the mill facilities and the current water supply system, the young engineer came up with the ingenious idea to install an overshot water wheel which derived its power from water flowing over the top of the wheel. This new wheel was reliable even during the months of low water flow, thus ameliorating the efficacy of the water supply system and speeding up the production process. With the water power issue settled, Marin now needed to concentrate on a bigger problem – acquiring wood.

It was a beautiful spring Sunday morning when he decided to go for a ride northward of the Cornaro estates and take a look for himself at possible forest areas to be exploited for timber. With the warmth of the sunshine on his face, he rode nonchalantly through the estate vineyards, the orchards with the citrus fruit trees, and the olive groves.

He headed farther north marveling at the cyclamens[1] and the tulips which came in all shades from deep violet and pink to pure white. They grew out of the ochre rocks, a color so much brighter on this sun-washed island than in Venice. No wonder Cypriots have celebrated the beauty of nature in spring, sprinkled so open-handedly on this floral haven, with processions of garlanded men and women in honor of Aphrodite and Adonis.

He drew in the reins on the top of the hill overlooking a secluded cove. He let his gaze rest on the panorama of the playful hide-and-seek of the golden sunbeams with the cotton white clouds in the otherwise clear azure sky that was reflected on the intense blue color of the Mediterranean Sea.

---

1 The island's national plant.

He wished he had brought his sketching material along. He missed having time to sketch almost as much as he had missed the sea and the feeling of absolute freedom when sailing toward the horizon with the salty, sticky sea breeze in his hair and on his face.

He was content with his work at the mill and the estates, but he couldn't help feeling tied down now and then. Once or twice, he managed to take a boat out along with his fishing gear and be all by himself. Swimming nude, becoming one with the crystal clear blue waters off the shore of the Episkopi bay, felt like returning to his lover's arms after a long journey. These were perhaps his only unperturbed moments on the island.

Marin had lost track of time in the serenity of the landscape, but he was aware of having left the boundaries of the Cornaro estates behind him. In the distance, he made out a mud-brick country house, half-hidden amidst the golden oaks, the junipers, the carob, and the olive trees, and decided to make the acquaintance of his neighbors. When he came close enough, he dismounted, tied his horse safely to the trunk of a mulberry tree by the porch, and knocked on the door, but there was no answer. The dwellers were probably out, he thought, and took to walking around the house.

He stood still as his eyes came to rest on a young woman sitting on a blanket underneath a lemon tree. The baby in her arms hungrily sucked on her swollen soft white breast. Marin was bowled over the image of the age-old mother-child bond in front of him that lazy, warm spring Sunday, scented with the perfume of the lemon blossoms. He dared not move.

Saturated, the baby let go of the erect nipple, turned her face to the side, still holding on to her mother's breast with her tiny hand. Satisfied, she closed her eyes in the safety of the familiar arms and surrendered to her lullaby, a tune Marin thought he recognized. He had heard one of his servants sing it to her infant a couple of times.

"Go to sleep, and I've ordered your dowry from Polis[2], and from Venice, your clothes and golden jewelry..." the young woman sang while rocking her child to sleep.

She hadn't yet covered herself up, and Marin did not think it proper to make her aware of his presence just yet. There was something erotic in her voice, he thought, or was that her bare breast exposed to the delight of his eyes?

The ginger half-breed that was dozing off by her feet must have sensed his stare, for he suddenly raised his head, jerked his ears up, and yapped at him. The woman turned her face around to see what the commotion was all about and in a protective motion, she held tighter onto her child. The dog took a few threatening steps toward Marin yelping even louder.

Not meaning to scare her, Marin took a step back stretching his open arms in front of him looking for the right words, "Fear not, *signora*. I just..."

---

2 Constantinople.

23

On board *CY433, 2011*

Lorenzo looked curiously at the picture-pretty coastal line as the A320 began its descent toward its destination and tried to imagine what Marin's first impression of this island might have been.

In a way, this vacation felt like turning a leaf. Searching for Marin came as a handy motive, but even if his quest remained fruitless, he intended to enjoy his stay to the fullest. He wondered if the flavors of Cyprus' cuisine were anything like the flavors Beth and he had discovered on Crete on their last trip together.

He would have to stop that, he thought. Associating everything with Beth was not helpful. He would have to let go, he reminded himself one more time. He stared at the wedding ring on his finger. He meant to take it off, but he had been postponing it for a year. *There's no time like the present*, he thought, removed it, kissed it, and kept it safe.

24

LARNAKA, 2011

At the travel agency, Marina waited a few minutes before she was shown in for the briefing session.

"I'm sorry I kept you waiting, but we had this urgent request for a conference with two hundred delegates. They had originally booked in Egypt, but with the current political instability, they thought it safer to move the conference to Cyprus. Anyway, regarding the Italian," he said, searching his emails and then looked up at Marina again. "I have already forwarded you his latest email."

"Yes, I got it. VIP package, no special or dietary needs, wants to discover the flavors of Cyprus. I've already prepared some itineraries for him to choose from – the focus on culinary tours. It's all here," she said, flicking open a folder.

The department head quickly browsed through the proposed outings and nodded. "It looks good. Like always. Check with Costas which car is available. Questions?"

"No, everything's clear."

25

1467

In the pandemonium of the dog barking, his horse neighing, and a donkey's braying, Marin stopped talking and looked down just in time to see a terrified blunt-nosed viper. He had been unfortunate enough to stand on its tail, and the viper sank its teeth into his calf in self-defense. Marin drew his sword and in a decisive move cut the reptile in two with its sharp blade, but, alas, too late. He looked up and saw the young woman placing her peacefully sleeping baby in her basket and dash to him.

"Hippocrates, be quiet! Sit!" she ordered, and the dog obeyed at once.

Marin felt nauseous. If it was the venom or his fear, he didn't know. He went down on his knees. A man of the sea, he had never been beaten by a snake before.

The woman reached him and freed her hair from her veil.

"*Signore*, sit up!" she said firmly.

She speaks Venetian, he thought, and did as he was told. "Is it venomous? Is there an antidote?"

"Yes and no," the young woman replied while tying her veil above the snakebite with swift, resolute movements.

"What?" Marin raised his perplexed eyes to her.

"Yes, it's venomous, and no, there's no antidote, but don't worry. I'll take care of your wound. It can be dangerous only if it's not treated at once."

Or so she hoped. Against her better judgment, she decided to move him into the house right away, for she did not possess the titanic strength to carry him alone later should he faint. Her curls smelling of roses fell on his face, as she placed his arm around her shoulders and said in an authoritative tone of voice, "*Signore*, help me carry you to the house."

Elena helped the stranger inside, rushed to fetch her baby, and came back to help him sit up on her bed. She quickly cut the garment around the viper's bite. She cleaned the already swelling wound and searched her herb cupboard which contained most of the 673 different kinds of aromatic and healing herbs that grow on the island. She tried to remember what her nana had taught her about snakebites.

She feared that the *Aristolochia sempervirens*[1] was not enough so she added some *Arum hygrophilum*[2] in the mixture she prepared. She applied it on his wound, tore a piece of a clean bed sheet, and bandaged it. Only then did she realize the state of her tunic and rushed to make herself decent even though the stranger was already demonstrating symptoms of hypotension shock.

Before long, he fell into the arms of Morpheus. In his restless sleep, the young man murmured "at arms" and "pirates, starboard" and a few other words Elena couldn't make out. She sat on the bed by his side as he was drifting in and out of consciousness and spoke tenderly and reassuringly to him, holding and patting his hand.

Every now and then, Elena removed a lock of his dark hair and checked his temperature with the back of her hand. When his forehead felt hotter, she undressed him from the waist up, and tried to bring his fever down with cold compresses. She let her fingers slide on the golden St. Christopher hanging from his neck for a moment before she turned him on his side to wash his back. She frowned noticing a nasty scar on his right scapula, probably caused by a dagger.

She turned him on his back again and stared at his pale, yet handsome, face, suddenly becoming aware of the whole year that had passed since her husband's tragic death in the hands of the pirates on his way back with goods from Syria. That was the day that changed her life. In one day, her husband lost his life and their fortune. In the days that followed, their house

---

1 Commonly known as creeping vine.

2 Commonly known as green arum.

in Limassol was lost to the loan sharks her husband had borrowed money from for this trip. Elena barely managed to save nana's country house. His parents accused her of being cursed and blamed her for their son's death for reasons beyond her ability to comprehend or accept and refused to have anything to do with her again. Bitter with their unjust treatment, Elena decided not to let them know she was expecting his child.

In front of the wooden crucifix that hung on the wall by the bed, the young mother lit a *kandili*[3], burned incense in a censer, went down on her knees, and prayed for the unknown young man before she got up to check on him and her baby again.

When his sleep finally became peaceful, she placed his white shirt and his black leather waistcoat with bronze nails, the heads of which were covered with a golden leaf, on a chair. She moved toward the door but stopped in front of the mirror and broodingly looked at her reflection. She picked up the ivory comb, combed her messy hair, and walked outside into the freshness of the rose-scented evening followed by Hippocrates. She leaned against the trunk of an old lentisk at the top of the cliff and gazed at the iridescent waves rolling lazily onto the moonlit shore. She concentrated on the gentle breeze, trying to cool down the uninvited heat inside her.

In the past year, she had been living almost like a hermit. Not only because she feared Ioanna's grandparents might try and snatch her baby away from her should they find out about her, but she also preferred it that way. Living alone in the wilderness gave her a sense of freedom she could not have enjoyed if she had remained in the 'civilization' of Limassol. She had spent most of her life in the wilderness. It didn't scare her. Her heart skipping a beat when she was around the stranger did.

---

3 A glass container that is filled with water, olive oil, and a wick usually placed in front of an icon.

26

Larnaka International Airport, 2011

Lorenzo waited patiently until the fasten seat belt signs went out, unbuckled, picked up his black blazer from the empty seat next to him and stepped on the aisle. A friendly flight attendant bid him goodbye. He smiled at her and walked in line with the other passengers on board. He got onto the bus that took them to the airport building and quickly cleared the passport control along with all European Union citizens and walked to the baggage claim area.

With a small piece of luggage in his hand, he walked through the 'nothing to declare' lane and passed through the sliding doors where people were waiting to welcome their friends and relatives. Among them, a few travel agency representatives were holding up placards with passengers' names.

He spotted his name on a placard in the hands of a young woman with an elongated neck and rich dark brown curls that occasionally fell naughtily in front of her eyes and which she would push away playfully.

She looked svelte in her black boots, black jeans, a fitted white blouse, an unbuttoned black vest with fine silver stripes and a black hat. She couldn't have been more than five foot five but must have felt comfortable with her height, Lorenzo thought observing her flat boots. She stood patiently watching the passengers walk through the sliding doors and waiting until someone would react to the name she was holding up.

Lorenzo walked up to her. When she met his gaze, she flashed a radiant smile at him that made her eyes flicker.

"*Signor* Zanetti?" she asked for confirmation when he came to stand in front of her.

She looked small next to him but with curves in all the right places, he figured.

"Yes, I'm *signor* Zanetti." He took the hand she was offering him, surprised at how firmly the soft hand with the slim, long fingers shook his.

Marina removed a curl from her eye and lifted her chin so as to look at him properly. She wondered whether she should reply in Italian but then decided against it. "Welcome to Cyprus, Mr. Zanetti. I hope you had a pleasant flight."

"Just some turbulence, but it was all right. Thank you." He shifted his vision from one eye to the other and down to the bridge of her delicate nose on her fresh face.

"My name's Marina and I'll be your guide during your stay in Cyprus. This way," she said, gesturing for him to follow her to the exit while wearing her professional smile.

"It's a pleasure to meet you, Marina."

Marina! His Italian accent prolonged the vowels a bit more than in Greek. It was as if he almost sang her name, she thought.

"I believe we have the same last name," he ventured as they walked out of the building. The chilly wind stroke against their cheeks, and Lorenzo smoothed his hair.

"Yes, we do. My last name's Zanettou, but that's just the Greek ending for genitive to indicate the family origin – usually for women," Marina elucidated him.

"Is this a common name in Cyprus?"

"Um... Not really," Marina replied while unlocking the car which was conveniently parked by the entrance.

"Are you of Italian origin?" he asked as she was opening the car boot for him to put his suitcase in.

"I couldn't honestly say." Just then, Marina realized she had never had a second thought about her last name. It was just the name her family went by.

"Did you know that Zanetti is a typical Venetian name?" Lorenzo asked while closing the car boot.

"Uh, no."

"Sometimes 'Gi' was changed into 'Z' in Veneto. Already in the fifteenth century, the Venetian form of Gianni was Zane or Zuane, for instance, just as Zorzi was for Giorgio."

"That's interesting," Marina said, glad she hadn't switched to Italian.

27

1467

Marin relaxed in his sleep, as an angel sat guard by his side whispering words of comfort. Several hours later, he awoke with the scent of the burned incense in his nostrils. With some effort, he opened his languorous eyes and tried to gather his bearings. Hippocrates, who stood guard by him all night, rested his snout on the bed and licked his fingers. Marin smiled faintly and patted his head.

He looked around the long narrow chamber with a chimney in one corner and a loom in another. It was a humble, plainly whitewashed place, sparsely furnished and adorned, apart from a vase decorated in geometric shapes on a table covered with an embroidered tablecloth and a crucifix on the wall. What astounded him as incongruous, however, were the two books on the shelf: The *Holy Bible* and *The Great Book of Herbs*.

The door opened and a young woman came in, uploaded a bucket filled with water, and disappeared into the adjoining room to feed the silkworms with the mulberry leaves she had just collected. She was so small with one of those ageless faces that she could even be mistaken for a girl, he thought, when it suddenly all came back to him.

With agile feline movements, the young woman came back into the room and said 'good morning' in a rather formal tone of voice, but with warmth in her eyes.

Stupefied, Marin looked out the window only to become conscious of the dawn breaking. He had spent the entire night there in her house! Jacomo must have organized a search party by now, only he hadn't told anyone where he would be going. He rested his head on the pillow again.

"Good morning," he said, half closing his heavy eyelids, with a dim smile on his lips and the sweet memory of her bare soft white breast as the baby was enjoying her nipple.

Elena came and stood by the bed and placed her hand on his forehead. "Your temperature's back to normal. You can get dressed now," she said in an authoritative tone of voice and Marin looked at her taken aback. She handed him his clothes, making an effort not to stare at his strong torso, and Marin slipped back into his shirt.

"Where am I? Who are you?" His voice sounded a bit weak even in his ears.

"You're safe. Best you don't talk much."

Marin had gotten used to giving orders to serfs, not taking them. He looked at the serene look on the young woman's face, trying to figure out why she felt so comfortable ignoring a master's questions. She walked to the cauldron while Hippocrates lay back down by the bed. She was wearing her hair up this morning, and Marin's eyes rested on her slim bare neck as she was pouring some liquid into a cup. In the familiarity of her home, she obviously didn't deem it necessary to wear a headdress.

"Drink this. It will invigorate you," she said as she was offering him a cup.

Marin wondered where her husband might be. He didn't see him the day before, and there was no sign of him now. He took a sip of the herb-scented broth and grimaced. "It's too salty," he complained.

"So it should be. All of it," she said strictly.

Marin looked up at her wondering one more time who this mysterious woman was.

"If I drink up, will you tell me your name?" he challenged her and saw the corners of her mouth form an unforced smile.

"Only if you drink all of it," she played along. Obediently, he drank up, and his face was contorted with disgust. She took the empty cup, and Marin grabbed her hand gently.

"I kept my end of the bargain," he insisted.

The young woman gave him a smile more mysterious than Mona Lisa's. "And I will keep mine. I just didn't say when" came back the unexpected reply.

She broke free from his grip and placed the cup on the table. Marin tried to disguise his disbelief.

"Where's your husband?"

The moment the question slipped out, the young Venetian realized he was almost rude to his savior and hostess. It didn't much matter, he thought. She was just another serf.

He clasped his hands on the pillow under his head and let his eyes glide on her lightsome posture and her unassuming features. She wasn't a ravishing beauty, but she was, in her own quiet way, quite pretty, especially when she smiled. Her broad forehead gave away an analytic mind, and the penetrating gaze of her almond-shaped brown eyes saw right through him, Marin thought, and wondered if she was a witch. After all, she lived like a recluse in the woods. She knew a lot about herbs, and she had that mystic expression on her face.

"*Signore*, your family must be desperately looking for you. I think you should ride back soon. I'll go get some eggs to make you breakfast."

He sat up in bed. "They can wait a while longer... Listen, I'm afraid we started on the wrong foot. Can we start over?"

She eyed him somberly as if weighing his words and finally nodded her consent.

"*Signora*, may I introduce myself? I'm Marin Zanetti, supervisor at the Cornaro sugar mill and estate. You have saved my life, and now I'm at your service," he said affably.

As if to introduce herself, too, the baby gave out a cooing noise to let them know she was awake. Elena lifted her from her cot and appeased her. The baby rubbed her little cheek against hers and was quiet again. "I'm Elena, and this is Ioanna," she said softly.

Hippocrates woofed and their hands touched momentarily, as they both instinctively stretched their arms to caress him. The half-breed wagged his tail happy to be the center of attention. "And this is Hippocrates," Elena said, smiling fondly at her dog.

28

2011

Lorenzo walked to the front door of the car when he heard her ask politely, "Uh, Mr. Zanetti? I don't suppose you would like to drive, would you?"

"Uh... No, not really."

"Well, perhaps you would like to come this way then. You see, in Cyprus, we drive on the left. One of the remnants of British colonialism," she explained.

Lorenzo looked at the steering wheel through the car window and then at Marina. "Right! I'm afraid I don't know much about Cyprus, but I do expect to leave the island more enlightened." An embarrassed smile crossed his face, and Marina couldn't help smiling back.

"When was Cyprus a British colony?" Lorenzo asked, looking out the car window as the sun was trying to find gaps between the clouds.

"Between 1923 and 1959, but the British had been actually ruling the island since 1878."

"How's that possible?" he wondered out loud.

"When Russia won the war with the Turks in 1878, the British saw their economic interests - that is the newly built Suez Canal - threatened. In an agreement with Turkey, they rented the island, but when Turkey allied itself with the Austro-Hungarian Empire at the outbreak of World War I, the British nullified the treaty and annexed Cyprus. With the Treaty of Lausanne in 1923, Turkey relinquished all claims to Cyprus, and the island became a British Crown colony," Marina elaborated briefly.

Lorenzo found the sound of her calm voice soothing and the soft way she pronounced *s* charming. "And after '59?"

"Cyprus became independent, but Turkey, Greece, and Britain remained guarantor powers. Some independence, huh!" Marina said, getting onto the A5 toward Lemesos and turned on the windshield wipers, as it began to drizzle again.

Lorenzo looked at her, wondering if he could give an account of Italy's history in a nutshell - probably not. History had never been his favorite subject at school - the break was. He glanced at the sun setting hastily in the distance ahead.

"We must be heading west," he observed.

"Yes, that's right. The Intercontinental is in Pafos in the west. Well, halfway between Lemesos and Pafos. It's one of our nice hotels, and I'm sure you will find the view breathtaking."

"You have just put my expectations high," Lorenzo said challengingly.

Marina locked eyes with him for a fleeting moment, offered him an evanescent smile, and focused her gaze on the road again. "You won't be disappointed. But you won't be able to see much today. It will be dark by the time we get there." Marina checked the mirror before overtaking another truck in the rain.

Lorenzo scrutinized the woman with the girlish face next to him. She seemed confident behind the steering wheel, and that was comforting. All this driving on the left would need getting used to. When he was in London, he preferred to let Beth do the driving. She knew her way around better anyway. He shook his head as if to chase the thought of Beth away.

The light wind intensified and eventually turned into storm as the blue velvet of the evening was spreading around them.

"Is it always so windy?" he broke the silence.

"Not really. Homer referred to Cyprus as *anemoessa*, from *anemos* the wind, as winds occasionally come inland even from as far as the Sahara, but it hardly ever gets this windy." She turned and faced him. She hadn't noticed before, but her client was quite good-looking. He smiled warmly, but there was a touch of melancholy in his smile, she thought.

Soon the rain turned into a downpour, and Lorenzo considered it wiser to keep quiet and let his guide concentrate on her driving. At least, she limited the overtaking of other cars. It was raining buckets, as they got onto the A6 toward Pafos, and he wondered whether he should suggest pulling over, but Marina reduced speed and kept going intrepidly.

A good half hour later, the car came to a complete halt at the portico of the Intercontinental Aphrodite Hills Spa and Resort. Marina opened the car boot as a friendly porter came closer, welcomed them, picked up Lorenzo's baggage, and had it taken to his room.

As Lorenzo was getting out of the car, Marina said, "I'll park the car and come and find you in the lobby."

Lorenzo nodded and walked inside, and Marina looked for a parking space adjacent to the entrance. She locked the car and ran to the hotel with the wind blowing the torrent at her from all angles. The porter opened an umbrella and ran to her, but a big gust of wind blew her hat away and turned the umbrella inside out. She ran after her hat with the cold rain slapping against her cheeks and rushed to the entrance, but the drenching power unleashed onto her left her soaking wet.

When she finally reached the portico, she removed as much rain as possible from her clothes, ran her fingers through her hair, and willed any blasphemies out of her mind. She lifted her chin, straightened her back, and walked to the lobby where he was waiting for her.

29

1467

Marin got on his horse, raised his right hand to salute mother, child, and dog, and rode down the declivity to the Cornaro estates, with Elena's image etched in his memory and a million questions about her springing to mind.

The sun was high up in the sky when he finally made out the estate groves and vineyards in the distance, and he held tighter onto the reins. He suddenly felt somnolent and thought of dismounting but decided to ride on. Luckily, Nikeforos, his friend and stable caretaker, was in the vicinity, saw him afar, and rushed to him.

"What in God's name?" he said when he reached him. "Let me help you, Master Marin. Everyone's out there looking for you."

He helped him ride back and get down the horse. He supported him up the stairs to the terrace with the terrazzo[1] designs and into the mansion.

"I'm fine," Marin said feebly. "I've been bitten by a serpent. I just need to rest."

His words wreaked havoc amongst the female servants in the house, who hurried to carry him to bed, while Nikeforos dashed to Dr. Brusco's practice. Marin closed his eyes and only opened them again when the doctor was examining him.

The old man looked at him and shook his head. "You're a very lucky man, *signor* Zanetti. Whoever treated your wound saved your life. Blunt-nosed viper bites, although very rare, can be fatal if not treated instantly. I'll prepare an ointment for you to apply on your wound three times a day. You should be as good as new in a couple of days, although the swelling will take longer to subside. Try to get some rest now."

---

1 The Venetian art of putting to use discarded marble remnants.

30

2011

Lorenzo looked at Marina from head to toe and shook his head disapprovingly. "And I thought Cyprus is a sunny island," he said teasingly.

"Most of the time. It may seem hard to believe right now, but Cyprus can boast of three hundred and fifty days of sunshine a year. Today is just not one of them," she said, wondering at her serenity and broad smile.

As she walked over to the reception desk, Lorenzo couldn't help grinning at her effort to act professionally despite all odds. When she was done with the formalities, she joined him again.

"What time would you like me to pick you up tomorrow?"

Lorenzo rubbed the back of his head with his palm. He cast his gaze down at his elegant Italian shoes and shoved his hands into his pockets. "Marina…"

Marina, she tried to reproduce the exact way he said her name in her mind.

"You… you're all wet! Why don't you take the card key, have the floor valet dry your clothes, and have a shower if you like while I have an aperitif at the bar?"

It sounded really tempting, and, of course, she couldn't fail but notice she was dripping. "I'll be fine. Thank you. It's very kind," she hesitated.

"I insist. Look at you! You are soaking wet. You'll catch a cold. And then I won't have a guide," he said with laughter in his eyes.

Construing her spontaneous smile as assent, he pressed the card key into her hand. She thanked him and took to walking toward the elevator while he took a seat at the bar, took out his cell, and speed-dialed Sofia's number.

31

1467

Marin meant to pay Elena a visit bearing gifts and thank her for saving his life in the next few days, but unexpected problems at the sugar mill absorbed all his time and energy reserves. A dysentery epidemic, which reduced the number of able workers dramatically, was followed by a series of machine breakdowns causing production holdups. He was laboriously going over the mill books in his chamber late one evening, a fortnight after the snakebite, when Nikeforos knocked gently on his door.

"Come in," Marin said lost in his calculations, sitting at his desk, half-hidden behind a pile of log books.

"Master Marin, I see you are busy. Perhaps I should come back some other time," Nikeforos hesitated.

"It's all right, Nikeforos. What is it?" Marin looked up at him.

The two young men were the same age and height and could even be mistaken for brothers. The sympathy that developed between them from day one eventually evolved into friendship, and Nikeforos became Marin's most loyal man on the island.

"It's not important. It's just that you wanted me to keep you posted of anything that goes on around," Nikeforos started carefully.

"And?"

"And there are some new girls at the brothel in Limassol, and I thought you might want to know." Nikeforos hadn't failed to notice Marin's flings, especially on his evenings out to Limassol with Jacomo.

Marin snorted. "Thanks. I'll have that in mind." He stretched his arms lazily above his head and yawned. "Tell me, Nikeforos.

What do you know about the woman who treated my wound?" he asked casually.

"I don't know how come, but she was born *lefteri*. Some say she's a witch. Some say she's a healer. Sick people go to her for treatment. And she treats them all just the same, even if they have nothing to offer her... I just think it's strange for a woman to live alone in the wilderness."

"Well, even if she is a witch, she has to be a kind one if she treats people for free. Don't you think?" He smiled at Nikeforos who shook his head in agreement. "Is she married?" Marin finally asked.

"She's a widow as far as I know," Nikeforos replied, studying his master's face that resembled a sphinx. He waited discreetly for a moment and then wished him 'goodnight'.

When the door closed behind him, Marin smirked to himself. Funny, how he had no desire to be with other women. It was all that little witch's fault, he thought. Who knows what she had put in that broth she gave him? It must have been some kind of a spell on him because her image intruded his thoughts time and time again.

His eyes rested on the letter on his desk. He had received it from home that morning. He had it lodged in his shirt all day, but he hadn't had the chance to read it yet. Marin focused on the figures in front of him once more, determined to finish the work he had brought home first.

By the time he closed the ledger, everything was still in the house. Even the hound dogs were sleeping by the entrance. Marin took his boots and clothes off and slipped into his chemise. He picked up the letter and let his fingers slide on the fine paper from the Fabriano[1] paper mill.

Marin sat on his bed with the curtained corniced tester bed-

---

1 The only papermakers in Italy and the most successful in Europe at the time.

stead and rested his back on his pillows. He read the letter once quickly, hungry for his family's news. He then placed his left arm behind his head and read it over once again, more slowly this time, trying to visualize every detail described until his eyelids felt heavy. He turned and blew out the candle. He would take his time and answer them tomorrow.

32

2011

Marina inserted the card key into the slot, waited until the light turned green, pushed the door open, and for a moment, she stood stunned. She had never been inside the rooms before - only in the lobby to pick up or drop clients. The junior club suit was larger than her entire studio, she thought and giggled.

She took her boots off and her feet sank into the thick carpet. She let her fingers slide on the table with the fruit basket and the champagne on ice. With swift movements, she got undressed, put on the thick white all-cotton robe with the hotel initial, slipped into the matching slippers, asked the floor valet to dry her clothes, and headed for the bathroom.

She knew she was supposed to hurry, but the temptation to enjoy this luxury that would probably not reoccur anytime soon was too strong. She filled the Jacuzzi and tried all the jets. She then examined the little elegant *Korres* bottles one by one and indulged herself with a hot vanilla cinnamon bubble bath.

When she finally dried herself up, her clothes were laid out iron dried on the bed for her. She blow dried her moist underwear and her hat and checked herself in the mirror. It took her a while to bring her hair into shape. She refreshed her chocolate brown lipstick and her perfume and glanced at her watch. She had kept him waiting for over an hour, and he hadn't even had the chance to unpack yet. He was surely regretting his invitation, she feared, and walked to the elevator in brisk strides.

She spotted him sitting at the bar having a shot. He glanced at his watch and then toward the bar entrance and saw her walking up to him vigorously.

"I'm sorry I took so long. The hot water was a temptation I couldn't resist," she apologized. She still remembered the fights with George and how he loathed waiting for her.

He looked at her through half-closed eyes for a moment and then gave her a congenial smile. "It's all right. I had the opportunity to find out everything about *zivania* from Paul here." He pointed to the bartender with a slight move of his head, and he smiled back at them. Lorenzo chuckled.

"I knew it took women long to get ready. I guess I hadn't realized girls also need that long." He turned and faced her as his grin spread across his face. "*Scommetto che sono abbastanza vecchio che potrei essere tuo padre*[1]," he murmured under his breath, lifted his glass, and downed his shot, but Marina heard him all the same.

"I doubt that. I'm twenty-four, and you can't be more than thirty," she blurred out.

"You speak Italian well!" he said surprised.

"Only a little," she said, keeping a low profile.

"That's good… Anyway, I'm thirty-six." He met her disbelieving stare.

"Uh, here's your card key... And thanks again... So, I'll see you in the morning," Marina broke the embarrassing silence.

"Marina, it's almost nine. Why don't you join me for dinner?"

Marina's lips parted then shut again.

Seeing her hesitating, he added, "If there's one thing I hate, that's eating alone. Here I am, in a foreign country. I don't know anyone - anyone but you that is."

"Uh, this is very kind, but... uh..."

"Marina, do you know what I do for a living?" Lorenzo looked at her long thick eyelashes that he hadn't noticed before.

Marina was startled by his deep gaze for a moment but respond-

---

1 'I bet I'm old enough to be your father'.

ed wearing her professional expression, "Uh, no, I'm afraid I haven't been given this information."

"I'm a chef," Lorenzo said simply – as if that explained everything.

Hence the interest in the flavors of the island, she thought.

"I became a chef because I love the pleasure of good food. I bet the food here's exquisite, but it won't be a pleasure unless it is shared with someone." He stretched his arms and looked at her disarmingly.

She nodded and smiled. "In that case, thank you." The truth was that she was famished.

"I'll just go and have a quick shower first. Why don't you have a drink in the meantime?"

Without waiting for a response, he turned to the bartender. "Paul!"

Marina marveled at his speed of befriending people.

"Whatever the lady's having, charge it on my account, will you?"

"Of course," the bartender nodded.

She watched him walk away, took a seat at the bar, and ordered a dry martini. She picked a salmon vol-au-vent from the silver tray that Paul placed in front of her.

33

1467

Elena beckoned to the sad-faced young boy to follow her to the window where the light was better, and told him to roll up his sleeves. The young woman lifted the boy's arms and examined the red and white hues of scaly patches.

She looked up at his worried mother and said, "Don't worry. It's just psoriasis. It's not pretty, but it's not lethal, and it's not contagious. I'll prepare something to rub on his skin twice a day."

The relieved mother fondled the boy's hair. "Everything's going to be all right. Elena will fix you," she said confidently and smiled at him, and a faint smile cracked on the boy's lips for the first time that day. He observed Elena curiously as she prepared a mixture of olive oil and oregano oil in a little jar that she gave his mother.

The woman took a small red glazed pot of honey out of her apron pocket and put it in Elena's hands. "Thank you, Elena. God bless you!"

Elena smiled and watched them disappear. She went down on her knees in front of the wooden crucifix on the wall. She thanked the Lord for sending her a boy she could cure. She always felt sick to her stomach when there was nothing she could do for the people who sought out her help. She had seen so many people die she would have thought she would be immune to the pain of loss and helplessness by now. She said her prayer including the stranger's safe return to his home. She rose to her feet and checked on Ioanna who was playing with her *puppa* [1] on the blanket on the floor.

Being a Wednesday, a fasting day, Elena put some bulgur wheat in a cauldron with some water to boil. She rinsed the mallows

---

1 A doll made of rags.

she had picked earlier, chopped them, and added them to the bulgur wheat along with some bay leaves and rosemary. She squeezed the juice of a sour orange to add before taking the cauldron off the fire.

She dried her hands and came to stand on the porch for some fresh air. She lifted her eyes to the sky, and marveled at the bright orange color of the setting sun, turning into a pallet of pink fuchsia and violet shades. Another moon was about to succeed the sun and not a sign of life from the handsome stranger. She only hoped she had managed to save him.

She went back inside and took to collecting the cocoons of the larvae, to draw off the silk and spin it into threads. She needed to weave more silk and make Ioanna new clothes. It was unbelievable how fast she grew.

34

2011

A familiar smell penetrated his nostrils, as Lorenzo closed the door behind him. He grinned recognizing Marina's discreet perfume and closed his eyes for a moment letting it in. Without wasting time, he got undressed and under the shower. It took him less than twenty minutes to join her again at the bar. Unpacking could wait.

To her relief, he did not wear a dinner jacket. She would have felt way underdressed. But he still looked smart in his black Rogani shoes, black Gucci trousers, black leather belt, and charcoal shirt. Marina admired the ease with which he moved. In her stereotypical understanding of his profession, a chef succumbs to gluttony and flirts with obesity - nothing like his athletic figure. Let alone at the age of thirty-six, which was close to middle age in her book, considering that the average life expectancy for men in Europe was seventy-six.

He signed the check Paul presented him with and offered her his arm to help her climb down the stool asking, "Shall we?"

Marina accepted his assistance, enjoying his attention.

"Have you had dinner here before?" he asked while escorting her to the *Leandros* à la carte restaurant.

I wish! "Uh, no, this is the first time."

"Good. Then this is a first-time experience to share." He gave her a beaming smile.

At the entrance, a waiter rushed to show them to a table.

"Thanks. I got this," Lorenzo told him and pulled the chair out for her.

I can get used to this kind of treatment, Marina thought. George, who had grown up with the egalitarian doctrines of communism, always laughed at the aristocracy relics, as he called them. She had long suspected that this had little to do with communism. It was not more than a sad excuse to avoid treating her gallantly. She quickly sent the thought of George to the back of her mind.

Marina had a quick look around at the stylish decor. A smiling waitress gave them the menus, and Marina browsed through hers. She looked at the prices and the dish descriptions with the exotic names and the fancy ingredients and opened her eyes widely before raising an eyebrow. "I suddenly don't feel very hungry," she lied unconvincingly and heard him snort gently.

He found her expressive face irresistibly refreshing. Lorenzo suggested, "Perhaps I could help you choose," and Marina was thankful. "Do you usually prefer fish or meat?" He enjoyed her futile effort to mask her embarrassment with a smile.

"I don't mind either way. Just don't order anything that needs more than a simple cutting, please," she said in a low conspiratorial tone of voice.

Lorenzo gave an amused smirk. "I think I can handle that. Do you trust me?"

"I trust you more than I trust myself ordering," Marina replied and that was the plain truth.

When the waiter came, Lorenzo gave the order, sea scallops served with a five spiced almond butter sauce with chives, topped with a melon salad and pea tendrils as an appetizer and beef tenderloin, rare for her and blue for him, with a pan roasted vegetable Napoleon as entrée. Out of the corner of his eye, he noticed her observing him undisturbed. He accepted the sommelier's suggestion for a local cabernet sauvignon to accompany the beef but decided to go for an imported Riesling Auslese with the scallops.

Marina was glad he ordered without showing off he was a connoisseur. She just wished she knew more about gourmet cuisine and wine.

When their Riesling was served a few minutes later, Lorenzo raised his glass. "Here's to my beautiful guide who's going to teach me how to appreciate Cyprus."

Talk about putting expectations high, Marina thought, raised her glass, and rewarded him with a smile for the compliment.

"Your turn now to make a toast," he encouraged her.

Her eyes turned up and to the left in an effort to draw ideas from the creative hemisphere of her brain. "Here's to my..." *handsome*, she thought but didn't say it, "Italian client who's going to teach me how to appreciate good food." At that point, she had no idea how close she had hit home.

"That is a challenge I'm willing to rise to," he said with an enticing smile.

Lorenzo glanced around at the discreet colors of the ambiance and the flickering candle light shed on her features. The waitress appeared with their scallops, presented the dish, and left quietly.

"Enjoy," Marina said and took a bite of her tender scallop. "Mm..." she moaned impulsively while closing her eyes fully concentrating on her taste buds. "This is good," she offered her layman's view of flavor and opened her eyes only to see Lorenzo studying her face. She quickly swallowed, turned to her wine, and downed it.

"Never regret the gastronomic bliss," he said, smiling fondly at her as a waiter approached and topped up their glasses.

Marina cleared her throat and casually changed the subject. "How come your English is so good? Most of my Italian clients are not so fluent."

"My wife's… was British. We met while I was working for the Intercontinental in London. She was a chef there just like me," he said with a touch of sadness in his voice.

"I'm sorry," Marina said, lowering her eyes.

"No, no. It's all right. You couldn't have known. She died in a car crash right before Christmas, just over a year ago… At least, Paola, our daughter, looks just like her."

"Do you have a photo of Paola?" Marina tried to keep the conversation light.

"Sure." Lorenzo bent closer to show her some photos on his cell, a move that sent a wave of his scent to her nostrils.

Marina looked at the girl's innocent, buoyant face. "She looks like a little angel! How old is she?" she asked, noticing the fading wedding ring tan line on his finger.

"Thank you. She's five… going on fifteen. Paola's class is going on a day trip to a farm tomorrow." He stopped himself short, fathoming that neither his dead wife nor his daughter were the most interesting conversation topics.

"I bet she's excited." Marina wondered why he looked tense. "I understand you have a special interest in local food and wine, so I have prepared a list of itineraries for you to choose from," she ventured after a few moments of awkward silence.

"That's great, but first I would like us to pay a visit to the Honorary Consul of Italy."

35

1467

Marin focused on the data he needed to draft the report for his uncle. By now, he had all the necessary information to put his idea for a cotton farm forward and was confident his uncle would be pleased. Production at the mill ran smoothly again. His efficient handling of the situation resulted in maintaining the production well within the average.

The need to secure lumber beyond their estates, however, was growing as the weeks went by. In the east of the estates, the land was controlled by their rivals who needed all the timber they could lay their hands on for their own production. The sea was in the south, and in the west there was flat land. Their closest neighbor in the north was Elena.

He figured that too many days had passed by to ride back just to thank her again. A business proposal was perhaps an even better excuse to visit her. It might, in fact, initiate a series of visits if he played his cards right.

The wood acquired from her land would give him a solution to present to his uncle. One thing he had realized about Andrea Cornaro from the onset was that along with the problems, he wanted to hear solutions, and Marin would hate to disappoint him.

"You are leaving!" Jacomo lifted his eyebrows. It was unlike Marin to leave the mill before the last worker did.

"Yes, you look after the mill. I think I've found a way to solve our timber issue."

"How about going to Limassol later for drinks and girls?" the albino foreman suggested with a crooked smile.

"I might be late," Marin replied evasively. *At least, if things go well*, he thought.

"Well, what about grabbing two serfs when you come back?"

He winked an eye at Marin who tried to disguise his disgust with a smile. For the young Venetian, who took pride in turning flirting into art, there was neither honor nor grace in taking a woman just because he could - a concept Jacomo was incapable of comprehending.

"As I said, I'll be late." He grabbed his hat. "Have a good one."

He closed the door behind him, still feeling Jacomo's piercing eyes on his back and already regretting his earlier escapades to Limassol with the albino. He shook his head as if to clear away the thought and took a deep breath of the spring-bouquet scented afternoon.

36

ROVIGO *2011*

"I'm sorry, Barbara. I don't think we can make it this time. Lorenzo's in Cyprus, and I'm looking after Paola," Sofia declined Barbara's dinner invite politely over the phone.

"Cyprus?" Barbara arched her eyebrows.

"Yes, he's at the Intercontinental, of course, where else? In Pafos." Sofia let the information slip through her lips.

"Oh, well. Perhaps next time then."

"Sure. It would be our pleasure."

Barbara hung up and stared at her phone.

37

1467

Marin unloaded a basket that resembled Amalthea's horn. It was filled with *haloumi*[1], sausages, and smoked meats in red wine with dry coriander. Two bottles of *mavro*, salt, spices, and sugar completed the content of the basket.

When no one came to open the door when he knocked, he walked around the house, like he had done that first day he had ridden out there, only this time he made sure he removed the grass in front of his feet with his sword.

"I see you've learned your lesson," he heard her tease him.

She was sitting in the thick shade of a walnut tree, removing little stones and other impurities from the lentils before storing them for winter.

"I'd be a fool if I didn't," he said, giving her his most attractive smile that she graciously returned.

"How's your leg?"

"Fine. Thanks to you," he said with a smile.

Hippocrates materialized out of nowhere and playfully stood on his back paws leaning on Marin.

"You missed me? You did? Oh, I missed you, too!" he said playfully while caressing him behind the ears, and Hippocrates was elated.

Elena tried to hide her smile, consciously avoiding looking up in his direction. Instead, she poured the last load of lentils into a little sack that Marin offered to carry inside.

"I've made fresh lemonade. Would you like some?" she asked with a faint smile.

---

1 Hard, salted, white cheese.

"Sure. And this is for you." He said, offering her the basket.

"It wasn't necessary."

"It's nothing compared to your saving my life. The doctor said you did a great job. It's just a way to say 'thank you' – even if a bit late."

He smiled apologetically, and Elena accepted it with a nod of her head.

He followed her into the kitchen and took a sip of the lemonade she offered him, casting a glance at the unpretentious, cozy, little place, while Elena took to tidying up the content of the basket.

"Did you make these wood carvings?" Marin asked with interest.

"That was a long time ago when I had … more time."

A life, she wanted to say, but she didn't want to sound like she was feeling sorry for herself. She was young and healthy and the good Lord had blessed her with a wonderful, healthy child, and she had her freedom and a place of her own. Most people had far less than that.

"Maybe one day, you could teach me how to carve the wood, and I could teach you how to sketch."

"We'll see," she said, wondering where he was heading and picked up her sewing work.

Marin cleared his throat and said "I did not come here today only to thank you." He waited a moment before he proclaimed, "I've also come here to discuss business with you." He searched her eyes, but her face revealed none of her thoughts.

"I'm listening, *signore*," she encouraged him – her curiosity triggered.

38

2011

When the sommelier left, Marina asked in a devil's-advocate tone of voice, "Isn't this wine tasting ceremony a bit overrated?"

Welcome to my world, Lorenzo thought and explained how tasting helps determine a wine's complexity, potential, and faults and then guided her through the steps involved.

"Pick up your glass and look at the wine," he encouraged her.

"All right, what am I looking at?" What aspiring wine connoisseurs always looked at before drinking was a mystery to her.

"Marina," he said passionately, "look at its color, its clarity, its brilliance. Hold it against the light and look at the intensity of its color."

Marina followed his lead.

"This cabernet was served at the proper temperature. See how it shines?"

"Okay, now what?"

"Now, swirl the wine in your glass by rotating your wrist, like this." He showed her how, but Marina twirled the wine too vigorously and sent it sloshing over the edge.

He smiled warmly, easing her discomfiture. "It's all right. It takes some practice. The trick is in the arm. You need to hold your arm still and rotate only the wrist." Very patiently, he gave her easy-to-follow instructions and concluded the tasting procedure.

"Your daughter is very lucky. You make an excellent teacher." Marina offered him a faint smile and cast her gaze on the stained tablecloth.

Lorenzo was pleased he hadn't bored her. Apart from Barbara, he hadn't flirted since dating Beth, and he felt rusty. *Not that this is a date*, he reminded himself, but he enjoyed the practice nonetheless.

"Cypriots have made wine for over five thousand years," Marina broke the silence. "In fact, Cyprus vines are considered to be among the oldest in the world. When vines in Europe were decimated in the 1850s by a plague of aphids, our vines remained untouched."

"To Cyprus vines!" he proposed with a smile.

Marina lost count of the toasts that night.

39

1467

"I would like to buy the right to use the timber on your land in exchange for a hundred sezins," Marin said, wondering if she had ever seen so much money in her life.

Elena studied his face for a while and said calmly, "Two hundred."

"Two… two hundred!" Marin's eyebrows lifted high up and came down again. Was she bargaining with him? She should have felt gratitude!

Ioanna raised her head in her cot, and Elena put her sewing work aside and lifted her.

"It is my understanding, *signore*, that the Cornaro have exhausted most of their timber which is essential for the production at the mill. No wood, no sugar. Am I not right, *signore?*" she said in the same calm tone of voice, wondering where she had come up with so much audacity to talk to him like that. Provoking a master's temper was not wise. She was only hoping she had not misread his eyes.

Marin looked at Elena, who was now making faces to Ioanna to entertain her, at Ioanna, who was enjoying herself, and back at Elena. He wondered if this woman ever stood still. It was hard to stay focused with her moving all the time.

"But the price you are asking is…" He stopped looking for the right word, but Elena was faster.

"What any other cavalier would have asked of you. Except there is no one in the vicinity, is there?" She met his gaze and offered him a broad smile.

Marin looked at her with renewed appreciation for her astringent remark. Indeed, it required a certain degree of chutzpah and backbone to confront him like that.

"I am offering to *buy* the timber on your land." His words sounded like an indirect threat hanging in the air. If it had been anyone else, he would have forced him to accept the hundred sezins for his own good, but he couldn't do that with her.

"As opposed to stealing it from me? I'm sure you could. I could only stop so many trespassers, but I don't think that would be necessary. Cavalier Cornaro is such a gentleman, just like you. I shouldn't deem it necessary at all."

How wrong he had been to think of her as some ignorant, helpless peasant in the wilderness!

"The thought never crossed my mind."

He smiled at her, and she shook her head in acceptance.

"One hundred and twenty," he then said for the mere sake of challenging her to bargain. Marin was beginning to enjoy himself.

"*Signore*, I'm just a woman struggling to secure her daughter's future - the same woman who struggled hard to save your life. But, of course, a man's life is priceless."

How could he argue with that? He bowed his head in defeat and said, "It's a deal." If his uncle opposed to the price, he would have to use his own savings. He hoped it wouldn't come to that. Then again, she was worth it.

"Two hundred sezins then it is, paid up front. Your men can start as soon as I receive my payment."

They shook hands, and Marin held on to her small hand a while longer. The discussion did not evolve as he had anticipated. Instead of her falling into his arms with gratitude, she bargained him for more than he would be proud to report to his uncle.

40

2011

"I don't think I have mentioned this, but I'm not the only member of my family who has visited Cyprus," Lorenzo said casually.

"Well, the number of Italian tourists has risen," Marina remarked politely.

"Uh... This was... a long time ago - about five hundred and fifty years ago." He met her astounded gaze.

"Wow!" Marina turned a look of pure curiosity on him. "How do you know of this visit since it was so far back?"

"It's just a family legend," Lorenzo started self-consciously. "Marin Zanetti, an ancestor of mine, apparently an astute entrepreneur, had come to great riches, or so the family legend goes, by trading products from Cyprus. Now, why he chose Cyprus I don't know. I tried tracing him in Rovigo and in Venice, but without much luck."

"I think I may know why he chose Cyprus. The successes of the First Crusade encouraged the Italian maritime republics, such as Venice, to trade in the Eastern Mediterranean. Cyprus benefitted from its position on the sea routes from the West, especially after the fall of Acre, or during the papal embargo on Latin merchants trafficking directly with Muslims. Goods changed hands in Cyprus, and merchants here acted as middle men. But, wait! You said your ancestor was here about five and a half centuries ago, so that must have been in the second half of the fifteenth century."

"I can't be certain, but Marin Zanetti was probably born in 1447. It would be interesting to see if I can find reference to him here, hence the interest in your name."

Marina stared at him, and he wondered if he sounded weird.

"My ancestor is one of the two reasons why I decided to come to Cyprus," he rushed to add.

"And the other one is?"

"Not quite as bizarre. Holidays, relax, fun, a change from my daily home-work-home routine. Not that I'm complaining. Paola is the sweetest kid, and I'm happy creating in my kitchen. For me, cooking is passion - a never-ending discovery of savoring blends of flavors. You know, one day, I'd like to cook for you and take you along to a journey of gastronomic ecstasy."

He spoke fervently, and Marina heard herself say, "I'd love that."

The waitress appeared with their beef tenderloin, and Marina enjoyed it quietly this time, but she did allow herself to close her eyes. When she opened them again, he was smiling widely at her.

"A chef's reward is the delight he offers. It's beautiful to see people enjoy their food as much as you do."

"Thank you for putting it so delicately... To get back to Marin, sugar was Cyprus' most profitable export crop from the fourteenth to the early sixteenth century. There were three sugar mills, one run by the Lusignan dynasty, one by the Knights Hospitaller, and one by a Venetian family – the Cornaro."

"Venetians! Could there be a link?" he wondered out loud. He now wished he had paid more attention to his history teachers at school.

"Caterina Cornaro married King James II in 1472, and the Republic of Venice annexed Cyprus in 1489. That was the acme of the Venetian influence on the island until the Ottoman Turks' invasion in 1570. Logically, the last quarter of the fifteenth century would have been a very good time for Venetians to develop enterprising activity in Cyprus."

"So he might have been involved in the sugar business," Lorenzo surmised.

"Perhaps… In the late fifteenth century, the sugar cane industry in the Mediterranean declined partly because of the newly established sugar mills on the Atlantic Islands, partly because of worker shortage caused by warfare or plague, and partly because of the increasing popularity of cotton plantations which were less labor intensive, hence more profitable."

"His successors might have made their fortune with cotton then," Lorenzo took a wild guess.

"Maybe. The discovery of the Atlantic trade routes caused the stagnation of the island's economy," Marina added broodingly.

"Still, they might have lived a happy life here for all I know," Lorenzo said with a smile, and Marina shot him a pensive glance. "You don't think so?" he challenged her.

"We're just speculating here, right? Life in Cyprus has not been easy, you know. Its geographical position has been both a blessing and a curse. On the one hand, its location is both geopolitically and economically important. On the other hand, the island's nine thousand years of history is a series of alternation of conquerors whose only interest has consistently been making profit at the expense of the inhabitants and the natural resources."

"Conquerors all over the world have only self-interest in mind."

"Yes, that's true. But can you imagine how unbearable life must have been during the Ottoman period, for instance, to make a number of Latins become Muslims in order to survive? If that were the case with your ancestors, it will be next to impossible to trace them."

"One can only try!" Lorenzo said and took the desert menu the waitress handed him.

41

1467

Marin visited his uncle in his office in the palace in Nicosia, in what used to be the Knight de la Baum's estate. When the Lusignan palace was destroyed in the Mameluke invasion in 1426 and King Janus was taken prisoner, the knight's estate was turned into the royal residence.

The meeting turned out better than he had expected. Andrea Cornaro seemed quite pleased with his report. Only when Marin mentioned the two hundred sezins, Andrea's gaze bore into him. If he thought the price was too high, he never said it. Instead, he gave Marin free rein to run the mill and the estates as he saw fit, as long as he kept the production up and running and the profits accruing. Marin even got the green light for his cotton project, too, and he was eager to set it up.

Andrea suggested having lunch together, but the meeting was cut short when the *bailli*[1] requested exigent audience with the Auditor of the Kingdom. Marin bid Andrea goodbye and headed to the stables, sauntering through the beautiful palace gardens adorned with marble statues, ponds with goldfish, water lilies, and fountains. It was a synthesis of infinite bright colors of flowers, citrus, olive, carob, and pine trees.

---

1 The Head of the Secrète, the king's central financial office.

42

2011

A waiter wished them goodnight, and Lorenzo and Marina walked to a nearby elevator. He glanced at the clock on the wall surprised to see it was almost midnight, and he insisted on walking her to the car.

As they stepped outside, Marina shivered in the chill of the night. Instinctively, Lorenzo wanted to rub her arms and keep her warm but thought better of it and held himself back. They reached the car, and Marina opened the door to the driver's seat.

"Thanks for dinner. It was just... great." She offered him a gentle smile.

Lorenzo took her hand and brought it to his full lips. "Thank you for a wonderful evening, Marina. Drive safely."

She flashed one last smile at him, wished him goodnight, and got into the car while Lorenzo stood there waiting for her to turn the engine on and drive away.

As Marina went down the slope toward the old coastal Lemesos-Pafos road, she lowered the car window and let the icy cold air in to keep her alert. She feared she had a drink too many. She played this unusual evening, her first fine dining with a handsome Italian client, over in her mind and wondered how she could possibly help him track his ancestor. She made a mental note to check out a few websites on the Internet when she got home.

Lorenzo walked back in, wearing a self-satisfied grin with his decision to come to Cyprus and his choice of a private guide.

43

1467

Marin reached the mud-brick house as the sun started to lower in the sky. He went up the three steps, found the house door open, and let himself in.

With her sleeves rolled up and the ribbons of her chemise undone, Elena was struggling over a cauldron with boiling water. She was so absorbed beating and spinning the laundry that was soaking in lye with a tree branch, which served as a washing *battoir,* that she didn't hear him come in.

"Here, let me!" he offered and took the tree branch out of her hands. Startled, she brought her hand to her chest taking a step back, almost forgetting to breathe.

"I'm sorry! I didn't mean to startle you," Marin said and smiled gently at her.

Realizing the state of her chemise, Elena turned her back to him without uttering a word, tied up the ribbons, and made herself decent. She dried the sweat from her flushed face with her sleeve. She then lifted the embroidered cloth, decorated with small shells at its fringes, from the spout of the terracotta jug with the vertical handle and the grooved neck.

The jug, along with the rest of the tableware, was part of the dowry her grandmother had left her. It was *sgraffito*[1] from the workshop in Lemba, on the outskirts of Paphos. The rough, dark red clay was decorated with floral patterns with tiny spirals, executed in very fine green and brownish yellow lines, using oxide of copper and iron.

She poured herself some water and gulped it down. "Thanks," she finally said.

---

1 The most common technique of Byzantine ceramic pottery.

"How long am I supposed to torture the laundry?" *and myself,* he asked a few minutes later feeling flushed, too.

"A couple of hours," she replied calmly.

"Seriously?" he asked, raising an eyebrow.

Marin, who had never been house-trained, had no idea how long the laundry usually took, but the conspicuous way she pressed her lips together made him suspicious.

"No, I've already done the first hour, so it's just one more hour for you."

"You're kidding, right?" he asked hopefully and watched her smirk.

She took the stick out of his hands, lifted a cloth, and offered her diagnosis.

"Done. How about you put your strong muscles to work and carry the cauldron and empty it outside while I hang the laundry?"

"Okay." Marin shrugged. He no longer found her unconventional manner strange. On the contrary, it fascinated him.

When the laundry was hung out on bushes to bleach in the sun and dry, he quickly got the money issue out of the way, eager to proceed without further obstruction with his conquest plans.

"Thank you, *signore*. You are a true cavalier – a man of your word," Elena said, taking the pouch with the two hundred sezins. She had half expected him to go back on his word.

She took to slicing the mushrooms she had gathered earlier on, and Marin picked up a knife to help her finish, so as to ultimately have her full attention. Elena cast him a curious glance that he pretended not to have seen. When she finally let the mushrooms dry outside in the sun, Marin saw his opportunity.

"I wish you would call me Marin, and I would like to call you Elena."

He looked deeply into her eyes and gave her his most seductive smile, but Elena held his gaze without returning his smile.

"*Signore*, I would like to get one thing straight. The money has bought you my timber - just that!" she said and assumed a posture of angry defiance.

Marin swallowed hard. In his scenario, they would be on a first-name basis by now, and before the night fell, she would be falling in his arms.

"Have I insulted you in any way, *signora*?"

He appeared offended. In his experience, women would be startled by such a direct offense and would smooth-talk him seeking reconciliation.

Elena needed a moment to think. She picked up her knife again and started removing the hard parts of the artichokes she had reaped in the morning, so as to preserve the hearts in olive oil and vinegar for the winter time.

"No, *signore*. And I would like to keep it that way." Elena wouldn't back down so easily - master or no master.

What? Marin tried to keep his wits about him. It irritated him that she wouldn't sit still.

"Does that mean we can't call each other by our Christian names?" he insisted in an innocent tone of voice.

"I'm afraid I don't know you all that well, *signore*." Elena kept looking at the artichoke in her hand.

"That is something I would very much like to change, *signora*," he played along.

"In the course of time, perhaps," she said warily.

It was high time for Marin's contingency plan. Out of his doublet, he produced a sheet of paper and charcoal.

"All I want is a friend. Someone I don't have to talk about business to. Someone I can relax with and sketch together, spend time together." He gave her his most irresistible smile.

Elena looked at the handsome young man through half-closed eyes. She could imagine that a master with his looks was accustomed to getting whatever he wanted. She also knew her chores wouldn't get done all by themselves while she spent the afternoon with him.

"*Signore*, I don't mean to sound disrespectful, but I still need to feed the animals, clean the stable, finish picking the oranges, make marmalade, prepare dinner, and give Ioanna a bath before feeding her. As tempting as your suggestion may be, I cannot shirk my responsibilities."

"Why don't I help you with the animals and the fruit picking, and you can take care of dinner and Ioanna. I'm sure the marmalade can wait until tomorrow."

Elena stared at him unprepared for such a response while Marin picked up two buckets and walked outside.

44

2011

Marina's heavy eyelids opened with difficulty as she reached for her cell to check the time. It was eight-fifty. Her eyelids shut once more before she sprang up in bed. Eight-fifty? Damn it! She would be late. Dashing to the bathroom, she decided to skip coffee. She hurriedly put her black jeans and boots on. She slipped into a red jumper she pulled out of her wardrobe and grabbed her jacket, her cell, her bag, and her keys.

She rushed to the car and took shortcuts through backstreets to get to the freeway, avoiding the morning traffic. She put her foot on the accelerator and fixed her gaze on the road. She was thankful that the A6 was unusually quiet and that there was no police speed control.

She exited onto B6 at Petra tou Romiou and checked the time. With a little luck, he might find her waiting for him in the lobby – that is if he wasn't the punctual type of client. *Most holiday makers aren't*, she comforted herself. She slowed down at the gate of the Intercontinental – Aphrodite village complex, raised her hand to greet the guard, and fished her ringing cell phone out of her bag.

"We missed you at the bowling game last night," Katerina cut to the chase – like always.

"I was working. I've an Italian client until the end of the week, remember?"

"What? You were working so late?"

Marina parked the car by the hotel entrance. "Well, he invited me to dinner, so I got home a bit late." She tried to sound casual about it.

"Dinner?" Katerina asked, expecting juicy details.

Marina locked the car and walked briskly to the entrance. "It's nothing like that. I just got soaking wet in the torrent and by the time my clothes were dry, it was already dinner time. That's all."

"Is he cute?"

"He's okay." Marina couldn't hide the smile in her voice.

"You like him!"

"Listen! I'm already in the lobby and late. We'll talk. Okay?" she said while her eyes scanned the lobby, but he was not there.

She breathed a sigh of relief that soon turned into a yawn.

"Rough night?" his voice came from behind her.

Marina turned on her feet and saw his clean-shaven face. "Uh, good morning. Did you sleep well?"

"Better than you, by the looks of it," he said, not failing to notice the black circles around her eyes. Lorenzo refrained from noticing that she had kept him waiting – again. "This way," he said as he stretched his arm to show the way and led her to *Eleonas* restaurant.

"The truth is I didn't sleep much last night," she said almost apologetically.

"Too much partying?" The words slipped out.

"Nothing as exciting as that. Too much studying."

She welcomed the smell of freshly brewed coffee in her nostrils. Her drowsy brain was craving for caffeine like the soil for rain after a period of extensive drought.

"You're a student? How many years does one have to study to become a guide?"

"Just one. I've already done that. I'm doing my master's now.

I'm defending my thesis on the twenty-first. Then I can start looking for a full-time job," Marina said while picking up a plate at the breakfast buffet.

"That sounds daunting. I wouldn't mind cooking for presidents or kings, but speaking in front of an audience…" He left his sentence unfinished and pinched some smoked salmon.

"It's okay. I'm used to it. Agoraphobia and guided tours don't combine well," Marina said, helping herself to various cheeses from the cheese platter.

"So being a guide is not your full-time job." Lorenzo pulled out the chair for her when they reached their table.

"Thank you. I like being a guide, but this is just a seasonal oc-cupation. Who's going to pay the bills all year round?" Marina asked rhetorically and gulped her coffee in an attempt to re-charge her malfunctioning brain cells.

"So there is no one in your life?" He topped her cup with more coffee.

"Thank you. No, not any longer."

"It can't have been long ago," Lorenzo observed, and Marina looked up at him.

"How can you tell?" She furrowed an eyebrow.

"I sense resentment in your voice." He took a sip of his coffee and held her in an examining look.

Marina shook her head. "Well, you know how it is when you've been best friends all your life and it's like destiny to be together, and then romance fades away, you grow apart, he starts cheat-ing, and all that… The worst part is that he doesn't leave my mom alone until she reveals my new phone number and address to him." Marina sighed. Why was she telling him all this? She took a bite of her freshly-baked croissant to stop talking.

She mentioned her boyfriend's cheating lightly, but Lorenzo noticed her wince and thought it wiser to change the subject. "You were right."

She finished chewing up and swallowed quickly. "About what?"

He gave an amused smirk at the sight of her raised eyebrow.

"The view from my balcony overlooking the Mediterranean *is* breathtaking."

Marina was grateful that he suavely saved the day. "It's Aphrodite's birthplace," she said and finished off her croissant.

"And I thought the twelve gods on Mount Olympus were Greek!"

He brought his index finger to the corner of his lips to show her there were crumbles on her face.

She followed his lead, cleared her throat, and said, "Well, according to Homer, Aphrodite was a Cypriot goddess. She was born emerging from the foam of the sea, right there where those rocks interrupt the endless blue of the coast. The moment she was born, a white rose burst into a flower as a welcoming gift from the gods and a message of love. According to mythology, when she ran barefoot to save her beloved Adonis, her feet bled. And that's how the first red rose appeared. In any event, a lot of sites and traditions here are associated with the goddess of beauty and love. Pilgrims would come from faraway places to worship her here, just as several centuries later pilgrims would make a stop here on their way to the Holy Land."

He flashed a smile at her. "Is there a legend for everything here?"

"What can I say? Cyprus is the stuff myths are made of. We like to keep legends alive... This very same location is also associated with Digenes, a Byzantine hero. Legend has it that he was a frontier guard who kept the Saracens away by hurling that huge rock over there into the sea and destroying their ship."

"He must have had some extra-terrestrial powers," Lorenzo teased, looking at the large size of the rock.

"Well, it's a legend. According to another legend yet, Digenes's hand is imprinted on top of Mount Pentadaktylos which literally means five fingers."

"Let me guess. It has five mountaintops."

"Yes, it does. You are getting good at this." They locked eyes and laughed.

45

1467

Elena chopped some firewood for the *fourni*[1] in the yard and filled it with loaves of sesame bread, olive bread, and terebinth bread with a peel. She meant to have done that in the morning, but Ioanna kept crying, and she never came round to it. She then simmered some stew for dinner.

Humming, she picked some pink wild mountain roses to adorn the vase and to make rosewater for Ioanna's bath. The public baths were too far away. Elena would often wash in the stream, but for Ioanna, she used a large bucket as a tub. She then crushed some lavender, burned it, and the room was filled with a relaxing fume.

She checked herself in the mirror and anointed her face with a cream she had made herself and her hair with some perfumed oil. She had just undressed Ioanna for her bath when Marin appeared with the buckets filled with oranges.

He put them down and produced an amethyst violet tulip that he secured gently behind her ear. He took a step back and gave her a wide smile.

"Just beautiful!"

Elena was grateful Ioanna's cooing gave her an excuse to turn away from him. She lifted her up and checked the water temperature in the tub with her elbow.

"Need a hand?" he asked, kneeling right next to her.

Elena cast him an astounded, perplexed gaze. *A master who does chores and wants to help with children!*

---

1 A mud-brick oven.

"Just tell me how," he insisted and flashed a smile at her.

"Just put your left arm under her head and hold her tight from the underarm and wash her with your right hand," she said almost in a whisper.

She looked at the grin on her daughter's little face. She was obviously amused by Marin's little waves and splashing water around her. Unexpectedly, he turned Ioanna over supporting her chin on his arm.

"What are you doing?" Elena asked with concern and curiosity.

"I'm teaching her how to swim."

"Oh!" For the first time, Elena was speechless.

Marin studied her face. "Do you know how to swim?" Most men didn't know how to swim, let alone women, but he would have expected anything from her.

"Swimming spreads infections and causes epidemics!" she protested. That was the general belief, although her nana always thought of this as plain nonsense.

"If that were true, I would have been dead by now," he said and smiled at her.

Elena rose to her feet and brought a bed sheet to wrap her daughter in.

"I could teach you if you like. It's an amazing feeling!" he said, lifted Ioanna up, and placed her in her mother's arms.

Elena, who had always enjoyed the sensation of water on her body while bathing in the stream, found the prospect of swimming too exciting to worry about the proximity of his body. She thought it wiser, however, not to respond to his suggestion, at this point at least, and took to dressing her baby.

"Would you be so kind as to step outside, *signore*? I need to feed her now." Elena made an effort to keep her voice steady. She could use the time alone.

"Why? It's not like I haven't seen you before." He found her jumpiness at the words of intimacy amusing.

"You make a wonderful picture the two of you. There's nothing to feel embarrassed about. Actually, I'd like to sketch you if you allow me," he encouraged her. He hadn't met a woman yet who did not feel flattered at the thought of being sketched.

The last thing Elena had expected that day was for the hand-some stranger to show up at her doorstep again, asking to sketch her feeding her baby. "*Signore*," she started to say, but Ioanna was getting impatient searching for the nipple that would still her hunger.

"I think she's hungry," Marin said, enjoying himself.

He grabbed the piece of paper and the charcoal he had brought along and took a seat at the table. It was obvious to her that he was as determined to sketch her just as Ioanna was in her quest for her mother's milk. She looked at Marin, who raised his open palms in front of him as if asking what she was waiting for, and then at her daughter who was getting agitated. She turned her back to him and took to feeding her baby.

Patiently, Marin grabbed his chair and took a seat a few paces further away so as to sketch her profile. Elena never lifted her eyes to him. With the adrenaline pumping the blood faster through his veins, he observed every single detail about her un-disturbed. At first, his hands shook slightly, but as he started to draw the first lines on the paper, he relaxed fully. He worked with fast movements setting the outline of her profile first, and then taking it more slowly, he refined the details of her facial ex-pressions. It suited him just fine that she wouldn't look at him. It would have made him nervous if she had.

He was adding the final touches when she put Ioanna in her

cot and made herself decent with her back turned to him. She walked up to him, but he hid the drawing playfully.

"Not yet, Elena. You have to be patient."

He had said her name a hundred times when he was alone, but the intimacy of calling her by her first name still sounded exciting in his ears. He concentrated on his sketching.

She looked up at him as if weighing the whole situation and then took to busying herself with her knitting. Marin knew she could hardly wait. *Women*, he thought and smiled to himself. When he was satisfied that he had depicted her tenderness for her baby, he rose to his feet and came to stand right behind her. He placed one hand on the back of her chair, leaned into her, and stretched his arm with the drawing in front of her. He nuzzled her curls and closed his eyes taking in the smell of lavender, causing every muscle in her body to flex.

"You are very good, *signore*," she started casually. "You must have had a lot of practice," *drawing intimate moments of women*, she was about to say but managed to bite the inside of her cheek just in time. *How many have you drawn already*, she wondered pursing her lips?

If Marin had read between the lines, he didn't show it. He chose to simply thank her. Needing to put some distance between them, Elena got up and tasted the stew. Just then she realized that most of the ingredients she had used for their supper that evening had one thing in common; they were all highly aphrodisiac.

46

2011

They stepped outside the hotel and walked to the car. Marina lifted her eyes to the sky and said, "If the weather forecast is correct, it may only drizzle in the coastal areas today."

"Good. I think I've had enough rain for one visit... You should wear red more often," he added casually before getting into the car.

Marina cast a glance in his direction, murmured "thank you", and got in, too.

The car rolled toward the freeway, and Lorenzo glanced at his watch. "It's almost eleven now. Is it ten or twelve in Italy?"

"Ten. It's one hour behind," Marina explained as she was accelerating.

Lorenzo picked up his cell and held a short conversation in Italian, but Marina could tell he was speaking in a dialect. When he hung up, he turned to face her.

"That was Sofia, my sister. She's taking care of Paola while I'm gone. She actually takes care of Paola quite often."

Marina returned his smile, surprised by the effortless way he was opening up to her. "The two of you must be very close."

"Yes, we are. How about you? Any siblings?"

The smile on Marina's face faltered, and Lorenzo held her in an inquisitive look.

"I don't know," the unexpected reply finally came.

"What?" Lorenzo's eyebrows arched.

"It's complicated." Marina fidgeted nervously.

"Try me!" he encouraged her.

47
1467

Marin raised his wine goblet. "To my lady savior," he proposed and the corners of his lips went up in a warm smile that lit his eyes.

"Anyone would have done the same," Elena said, casting her gaze on the goblet in her hand.

"I'm not so sure everyone would know how. I, for one, wouldn't." He put his arms on the table and leaned forward. "Tell me, Elena, how come you know so much about herbs? How come you speak Venetian or can read in the first place? Most importantly, how do you get to live as *lefteri?*" Becoming conscious of his bombarding her with questions, Marin stopped talking.

Elena's lips formed an unforced smile. "Are you always so impatient?"

"Not really. I just want to find out everything about you." He looked at her intensely.

"Okay. But for every question you ask, I get to ask one, too. All right?"

Marin nodded his consent.

"Let's see. The herbs. Well, my nana spent half her life in the wilderness. She wrote down everything she knew from her mother about herbs, so that I wouldn't forget."

Marin wondered if that was a brief shadow of sadness he detected on her face. "So, your nana knew how to read and write, too!"

Extraordinary, he thought! In the middle of nowhere, women could read and write. How was that possible in a world of analphabetism where the vast majority of men were illiterate, let alone women?

"My turn now!" Elena had her own agenda.

"Sure, go ahead. I'm an open book. Ask me anything," Marin encouraged her enjoying himself. He was so looking forward to unveiling the mystery encompassing her.

"How long will you be staying in Cyprus? I mean, foreigners, especially merchants, come and go. What are your plans?" She was satisfied her voice sounded casual enough.

"I've done some trading, but I'm not a merchant, Elena. Like I told you when we first met, I'm the supervisor at the Cornaro mill and estates. The Cornaro have been here for a hundred years. So how long do I plan to stay? Quite long I'd say."

He knew he sounded evasive, but just then he realized he had no inkling. He only knew he would be staying for as long as Andrea Cornaro needed him. Was she worried about that, he wondered?

"So how come your nana could read and write?"

Elena took a sip of her wine to give herself more time to contemplate her answer and to prolong his hanging on her every word. She was enjoying his company and his attention. She hadn't dined with a man since the evening before her late husband embarked on a catastrophe.

48

2011

Marina ran her fingers through her hair and sighed. "My parents used to live in Vokolida. That's a tiny village in the Carpass peninsula in Famagusta district, in the occupied areas… I wasn't born then. My parents had a boy, Alexandros. I never met him. I don't even know if he's alive."

Lorenzo wasn't sure he understood what she was saying exactly. "What happened?" he asked gently and waited patiently until she was ready to continue her narration.

"When the Turks invaded my parents' village in '74, they were out in the fields, while Alexandros, he was nine then, was playing football with his friends in the schoolyard. They had to flee from the planes bombarding them and the soldiers closing in on them. My parents desperately searched for my brother everywhere, but they never found him. Not even later in the free areas through the refugee message exchange programs on the radio. Not through their endless pleas and petitions to the UN for the missing people. Nothing. No one could help us."

Her voice broke and she paused for a moment to recollect herself before she went on. "Somebody said he saw Turkish soldiers taking the boys from the schoolyard and forcing them onto a military truck that day, so we don't know what happened to them. We don't know if they shot them, or if they've been rotting in a Turkish prison ever since. We just don't know," she said with apprehension in her voice.

"That's terrible!" Lorenzo said sympathetically.

Marina shook her head.

"Do you have a photo of him?"

"No. You know, in '74 people were fleeing for their lives. Some walked tens of kilometers in their flip-flops and shorts just to get away from Turkish tanks. They didn't have time to take anything."

Talking about her missing brother always left a tart taste in her mouth, and Marina changed the subject after an awkward silence.

"See here? This exit leads to Episkopi, where the Cornaro sugar mill I told you about last night used to be, and the next one leads to Kolossi castle. Right next to the castle there still stands a part of the sugar warehouse of the Hospitallers."

49

1467

"Well? Is it a state secret?" Marin tried to lighten up the conversation, but Elena didn't smile.

"When nana was young, she used to live close to Aphrodite's temple in Yeroskepou. In Greek, *ieros kepos* means holy garden. It is holy because it has been linked to the worship of the goddess. You say Venus, but we call her Aphrodite. You know, in Greek, Aphrodite means emerging from the foam of the sea. Anyway, my nana, just like her mother and her grandmother before her, was a member of the secret cult of Aphrodite - hence the knowledge of herbs."

The mere notion that such a cult was still alive, even if just underground, excited his imagination. Yet a sudden, vague feeling of jealousy took him unawares. "You mean you've been initiated in these rituals?"

"My turn. Tell me about your family."

"My father is a galley captain, and my mother is... a beautiful person. And I've two brothers, twins, and two sisters," he answered quickly before pressing her to answer his question, "Have you been initiated in these rituals?"

Elena looked at him through half-closed eyes, weighing the flame in his intense gaze. "No, but I know about them." She offered him an enigmatic smile and went on. "When nana fell in love with a clergyman, she abjured the pagan customs and lived a Christian life for his sake. He was probably too high in rank to marry her. High-ranking priests cannot marry. In fact, he must have been pretty high in rank because he could read and write... Nana said he was considering rejecting his office and becoming a simple priest so as to be able to marry her, but she didn't let him, out of fear he would regret it some day. *He* was the one who taught her how to read the Holy Bible you see on that shelf. That was his gift to her. *He* was the one who bought nana her freedom. A compensation for not being able to marry her, I suppose. When nana realized she was carrying his child, she decided to keep it, a part of him I guess, so she came to live in the wilderness. He would come and see her as often as he could, but the plague took him early... Nana taught my mother how to read and write, and she taught me. My turn now! Tell me about your life here in Cyprus." Her voice lilted across the room.

"I sometimes miss my family in Venice, but other than that, it's great! I love what I do. Not just the running of the mill and the estate, but also the fact that I'm given free rein to start up new enterprises! It's like the sky is the limit, you know." His eyes sparkled with excitement as he gave her a full account of his daily routine.

"How come you speak Venetian?" he finally asked.

"I don't speak your language that well, but I understand a lot." Elena folded her hands on the table.

"You don't make as many mistakes as you may think. What strikes me, though, is that you use some words typical of Florence." He looked at her, wearing an inquisitive face. He decided to hear her out before jumping into conclusions.

"My father was a merchant from Florence, doing business mainly in Famagusta."

Marin's eyebrow arched.

"It was summer when one day, he was on business in the area. He lost his way and drifted close to nana's place. A snake scared off his horse, and he fell off, hurt his head, and lost consciousness. My mother found him and treated him. They fell in love, and before next spring, I was born... We had joyful moments whenever he came for a visit. My mother insisted upon learning his language and teaching it to me, too. It seems they had this plan. He was supposed to make enough money, marry my mom, and we would all go and live in Florence."

The corners of her mouth formed a bitter-sweet smile as she

took a stroll down memory lane. Elena looked up at him, saw the pensive look on his face, and rushed to add in her mother's defense, "That wouldn't be the first mixed marriage!"

True as that might have been, it was more often than not the case of people of the same rank, at the higher echelon of society.

"But they never married," Marin remarked softly. He knew of all the promises men would make.

"No, they never did." Elena's voice was now bitter. "When he stopped coming, my mother was sick with worry, fearing something might have happened to him. She even rode all the way to Famagusta all by herself to seek him out or find out news about him."

Marin wondered if Elena's mother had been that brave or that desperate and reckless. "And? Did she?"

"My turn!" Elena said assertively.

"What do you want to know?" His lips formed an enticing smile. This self-disclosure dance, which resembled the Dance of the Seven Veils, inflamed his brain and body with desire. He had always suspected she had an intriguing story to tell, but that was beyond his imagination.

"Mm... How was your life before you came to Cyprus?"

"I traveled the seas and saw many different places, people, and customs. I'll tell you one day all about it," he promised.

Ample anecdotes that he wanted to share with her sprang to mind, but there would be time for that later. She was already worried he wouldn't be staying. Too much passionate talk about the thrill of traveling to the corners of the world might scare her off.

"Don't you miss that?"

Elena had always wondered what lay beyond the sea. Her husband had promised to take her with him to Syria on his last voyage, but the pregnancy put an end to her travel plans. In fact, it saved her life.

Marin tilted his head to the side and snorted. "Sometimes." He tried to read her eyes, surprised at his need to reassure her. "I can live without it," he heard himself say. "Did she find him?" he repeated his previous question gently after a moment of silence.

Elena sighed. "No. Apparently, he met someone of his own with money and status. What chance did my mother have? Against all odds, she waited for his return. She was devastated when she found out that he had left for Florence with his new wife. At first, she refused to believe it. Then she got angry and later depressed. In the end, she faded away."

Marin watched her lower her eyes as if the memory were too painful. He tried capping her hand with his, but Elena pulled her hand gently away.

"How come you have that nasty scar on your shoulder?"

"How do...? When you treated my wound," he answered his own question shaking his head. "I've a pirate to thank for. Once, off the shore of Limassol, pirates assaulted the *Miramare*. Actually, I was lucky I got away with just a scar. We lost eight good men that day."

"I'm sorry," Elena said, considering how she, too, had suffered the loss of a beloved one in the hands of pirates.

"How old were you when your mother died?" he asked softly.

"I was just a child. My nana raised me. She spent the rest of her life blaming herself for everything. She was convinced we were being punished for her love for the clergyman. Even before I grew up, she turned it into her life mission to find a good husband for me to break the vicious circle... I hope she's now resting in peace. She died a few days after kissing my wedding wreath. I'm only sorry she didn't get to see Ioanna."

Marin refrained from asking about her marriage. He preferred not to think of her in the arms of another man.

"Aren't you afraid to live alone in the wilderness?"

Elena looked at his unsmiling face. "Don't worry. I'm safe. No one harms a healer... or a witch," she said lightly, but a deafening silence followed her words.

Marin shook his head with a look of concern. "Just be careful."

The Catholic Church hadn't launched a full-scale hunt against witches yet, but trials and deaths had already been recorded. At least, the *Bulla Cypria*, which declared the Catholic Church as the official church in Cyprus, made little impression on Cypriots who remained loyal to their Greek Orthodox faith and heritage.

Marin chewed on the last of his *soupouthkia*[1] and downed the rest of his wine.

"This was definitely one of the best meals I've ever had."

Elena knew she could do magic in the kitchen with her rich herb combinations. She also knew the humble dinner she could offer him could not compare to the lavish banquets at the Cornaro estate. Deep down, she felt flattered nonetheless.

"Thank you, *signore*. You are very kind," she returned the courtesy.

"I'm afraid it's late. I should best ride back now."

Elena didn't respond, and he rose to his feet. She ushered him to the door.

He held her in a tender gaze and asked, "Shall I pass by soon to discuss which trees to cut?"

She managed an evanescent smile and a 'yes' and held him in her line of vision for as long as she could as he walked down the steps and got onto his horse.

---

1 Crisply fried cubes of bread in olive oil, drizzled with carob honey and served hot.

50

2011

"Are the mills worth visiting?"

"The castle is, but there's nothing left standing of the mills to see," Marina said, shaking her head. "There are two sovereign British military bases on the island. The largest one is here," she went on pointing to the right. "It starts from Episkopi and stretches all along the coast down to Akrotiri until the port of Lemesos. At Akrotiri there's also the smaller of our two salt lakes. The other one is close to Larnaka airport. During the Lusignan dynasty, salt lakes were so valuable that they used to be a crown asset - that is until they were disposed of to pay for the war against the Mamelukes."

"Lemesos. Isn't this where you live?" Lorenzo asked a few minutes later as they reached the first bridge bypassing Lemesos.

"Yes. Lemesos is the second largest city in population but the largest in geographical size."

"Is that right?"

"Yes. Lefkosia is still divided – the last divided capital in the world. Lemesos is Cyprus' largest port, the heart of the wine industry, a tourist destination, and the city of entertainment. At the end of the Byzantine rule, Limassol was a small market town between the ancient cities of Kourion and Amathus. Basically, it grew after Richard the Lionheart destroyed Amathus."

"Why would he do that?"

"It was a fit of chivalric rage over the discourteous treatment of his shipwrecked fiancé, Berengaria of Navarre, by the self-proclaimed emperor Isaac Comnenus, in 1191... The city survived destructive earthquakes, Genoese and Mameluke rapacious forays, and pirate depredations. If you add epidemics, failed harvests, and the conquerors' harsh exploitation, it is no wonder that at some point during the Venetian Rule, Limassol shrank to a village, and its residents had to fight to maintain the right to have their own bishop. To cut the long story short, then came the Ottoman Turks who sold us to the British before we fought for Independence."

Lorenzo looked at Marina and realized he was more interested in finding out about her rather than the island. "What do you enjoy most about living in Lemesos?"

Marina shrugged her shoulders. "Fist of all, Lemesos is just an hour drive from Lefkosia, and a forty-minute drive from Troodos, Larnaka, and Pafos, the ancient Roman capital. I like the old part of the town where I live. It's the historical and commercial center - lots of stores, cafés, galleries. Most of all, it's just a short walk to the beach."

"Could you ever imagine living anywhere else?" he heard himself ask.

She turned and faced him raising an eyebrow.

"For instance, not by the beach? Or Cyprus?"

"Well, I love Troodos, especially a little village called Platres. Actually, Troodos is considered to be the best-preserved and most systematically studied ophiolite complex in the world. Abroad ... I've never thought about living abroad. I guess it would depend on where and on the circumstances." She shrugged and went on, "I love Cyprus and its beaches. I spent most of my life living by the beach. Kato Pyrgos, the village I grew up in, although not very popular with tourists, has beautiful beaches. But I spent six years inland, in Lefkosia. So I guess, yes, I could live somewhere else. Of course, it was comforting to know that the beach was just a half-hour drive away, so if I had to live somewhere else, I would like the beach to be within easy reach."

"You know Rovigo, the place where I live, is only twenty kilometers away from the beach and just an hour drive from Venice."

"That sounds nice."

51

1467

Despite devoting long hours to see the cotton plantation take shape, it only took Marin a few days to return on the pretext of inspecting the area for timber cutting. Elena was whisking the dirt away from the porch with a broom when she heard the tread of the horse. When she was sure it was him, she rushed inside. A minute later she was welcoming him at the porch, wearing a warm smile.

"Not busy today?" Marin returned the broad grin while tying his horse safely to the trunk of the mulberry tree by the porch.

"Not really. Just finished weeding and planting the summer crops, and I was just about to take Ioanna for a walk and look for herbs on the way. It's such a beautiful day!"

"Great, then we can choose the trees for lumber." He pulled something out of his saddle bag, climbed up the three steps to her, and handed her a dress for Ioanna and a cloak for her. "For you," he said smiling warmly, not failing to notice she took the trouble to paint her eyes in black for him.

"Thank you," she said, marveling at Ioanna's beautiful bright yellow dress and the fine cloth quality of her cloak. "You shouldn't have."

"I wanted to."

"And this is for you, to protect you during your travels," she said while fastening the leather strap for him from which a little wooden cross she had carved was hanging.

Marin took the little cross in his hand and admired its finesse. "Thank you. I'll always wear this."

His Glaucous blue eyes sank into hers.

Hippocrates interrupted the moment with his barking around them, eager to lead them into the woods. The humid, grassy spring bouquet hit their nostrils. The half-breed was jubilant to play fetch with Marin, who never failed to praise him each time he came back with the twig between his teeth, waggling his tail crackling branches in his path.

When they were done marking the last tree to be cut with an X, Marin turned to her and said unexpectedly in a husky voice, "Elena, say my name!" So far she had only addressed him as '*signore*'.

"What?" she asked in a voice that was barely a whisper.

"I want to hear you say my name. Say 'Marin'," he encouraged her.

She smiled at him, lifted her eyebrows in a swift jerky motion as she opened her eyes wide to gaze at him briefly. Then she dropped her eyelids, tilted her head down and to the side, looked up again, and gently said his name, "Marin!"

You can deny it all you want; you're falling, and I'm right here to catch you, Marin thought with a self-satisfied grin spreading across his face.

"Say it again," he said excitedly.

"Marin!" Her face split into a wide smile.

"Elena," he whispered with fervor, leaned into her, and Elena closed her eyes. Feeling his breath on her cheek, she awaited his kiss.

"Don't you think it's time?" she heard him ask, opened her bewildered eyes, and saw the laughter in his eyes. Marin did not even try to hide his amusement at her confusion.

"To teach you to sketch!" He produced paper and charcoal from his doublet.

Elena tried to hide her embarrassment. She lifted her face to the warm sunbeams, half closing her eyes to the light filtering through the top branches. "Here?"

"Why not?"

52

2011

They took the Kalo Chorio exit on the freeway and drove past the eighteenth century Roman-style aqueduct heading for the consulate.

"How can one trace his ancestors in Cyprus?" Lorenzo asked.

Marina tilted her head to the side contemplating. "Hmm... I made some enquiries when you told me you were looking for your ancestor's trail. Unfortunately, it doesn't seem to be easy. The department of land and surveys was established in 1858, and the first census took place in 1881. There are no official documents dating further back. There are, of course, some church records and chronicles of the time, but they usually have references to nobility only."

Marina pulled up on Stassinou Street, and a few moments later they were walking into the consulate. Only then did the thought occur to her that Boustronios's chronicle might shed some light on his quest, but she would have to hold that thought. The receptionist was already on the phone announcing their arrival.

The consul was very polite when he received them. Further to the vice-mayor's request, he had already contacted the Catholic Archbishop of Cyprus, requesting his assistance for a quick search in the church archives, given Lorenzo's limited time in Cyprus. As a personal favor to the consul, the archbishop had been kind enough to supervise the archive search himself. He would be getting in touch as soon as there was progress to report. If Lorenzo needed anything else, the consul would gladly be of assistance. He even offered to take them to lunch, but Lorenzo could tell he had urgent matters to attend to, so he declined graciously.

Lorenzo left the consul's office hoping he was gradually unwrapping Ariadne's thread. "So now we just have to wait and see what information the church archives might have on Marin Zanetti."

"It's a long shot, but in the meantime, we could browse through Boustronios's chronicle. I have a copy of it at home."

"Let's do some sightseeing since we're here. My ancestor is not the only reason why I came to Cyprus. Remember?" He flashed a warm smile at her, revealing his straight white teeth.

53

1467

"You can start by sketching this pine tree here," he suggested.

Elena made herself comfortable on a rounded rock. Marin came and sat right behind her and put the charcoal in her hand, holding her hand in his.

"Hold it like a wand. It will help you block in shapes."

The touching of their bodies and his gentle voice so close to her ear made her hand tremble at first, but she made herself focus on his instructions. She had never thought of this before, but sketching would be a very useful skill, she decided. She could draw the herbs in her herb book for Ioanna. That would be her legacy should anything happen to her before she could teach her everything her nana taught her.

Marin guided her through, adding details and appreciating light and dark values. He was letting her into an amazing new world, and Elena followed his instructions obediently.

"Let's see what you've done," he said and lifted the sketch, still sitting right behind her. "Are you sure you haven't done this before?" he teased her gently. Transfixed, Elena stared in his Glaucous blue eyes.

"Elena, you are so beautiful," he whispered hoarsely. "You have bewitched me. I can't explain otherwise this burning I feel inside, this urge to be with you all the time. I'm sick with love, and only you can heal me." Marin leaned into her ready to take her lips, but Elena tilted her head to the side.

"And the only way you could fall in love with me is if I used my love potions. Is that right?" Elena asked affronted and rose to her feet.

Marin looked at her taken aback and got up, too.

"Go home, *signore*, knowing that no dose of a love potion lasts longer than a week. If in a week's time, you still feel the same, you will know."

Elena gave him no time to reply. She strode to Ioanna, picked up the basket with the sleeping baby, and called Hippocrates to follow suit. Elena wasn't really upset with Marin. She just wanted to find a way to stand out from all the women he had come across.

Marin stood stunned, watching her walk away from him, lacking any smart response. Even his best line didn't work with her!

54

2011

They left the castle museum dedicated to ancient Kition, the birthplace of the stoic philosopher Zeno, which was founded by Mycenean traders in the thirteenth century BC and went ambling to the adjacent *Finikoudes*[1] promenade, lined with palm trees.

"What time period is described in this chronicle you mentioned earlier on?" Lorenzo asked while shooting photos of the beach.

"1456-1489 – the transition from Lusignan to Venetian rule. There's reference to a lot of important people of the time, such as Andrea Cornaro, who was the king's counselor and the one who engineered the king's wedding to his niece, Caterina Cornaro."

"The one with the sugar mill?"

"The very same. You know, this is perhaps the most exciting time in the island's history - full of intrigues and subversions."

Lorenzo observed her enthusiasm through his photographic lens. "You're passionate, aren't you?"

Marina raised an eyebrow, and he immortalized it in a snapshot.

"Excuse me?"

He lowered his camera. "You have passion for what you do." He looked at her through half-closed eyes. He then pressed some buttons on his camera and chuckled. "Want to see?"

She nodded, and he gave her the camera. Marina had a look at her raised eyebrow. "Busted. I'm afraid I do that a lot." She shrugged.

---

1 Palm trees.

"I think it's cute," he said, focusing his attention on her.

Marina cleared her throat. "As I said before about the chronicle, it's a long shot, but when we go back…"

"All in good time. Let's go see some sights and grab a bite to eat."

"Sure. We can go to Lefkara. It's not far, and it's on our way back."

"Lefkara?"

"Yes. The village is famous for its lace making and silver handicrafts. It used to be a favorite resort among the well-off Venetians during the Venetian Rule."

"What? No legend associated with Lefkara?" Lorenzo asked challengingly.

"You know, of all people, I wouldn't have expected you, who came all the way to Cyprus to hunt a dead ancestor just because of a family legend, to make fun of keeping legends alive," she teased him.

"Touché!" He offered her a warm smile that she spontaneously returned.

"Well, actually, there is a legend about Lefkara," Marina started timidly, and he gave her an 'I-knew-it!' smile. "Cyprus was on the Silk Road, and tradition says that in 1481 Leonardo da Vinci visited the village and took a piece of needlework to grace the main altar of the Milan Cathedral."

"Da Vinci - huh? Wow! All these stories made me hungry. I could do with a snack for lunch."

"Sure. Let's grab some *souvlakia*."

They took to walking back to the car.

"Not *souvlaki* like in Greece?"

"Ours is a bit different. In the pita bread, we also add tomatoes, cucumbers, and parsley along with the grilled meat."

"A healthy fast food idea!"

"Something like that."

They locked eyes, smiled, and got into the car.

55

1467

Marin rode back to the Cornaro estates, furious at her turning him down. The servants got discreetly out of his way as he was helping himself to a bottle of *zivania* and a tray of *tsamarella*[1]. He disappeared in his quarters and kicked the door close.

He strode up and down like a caged beast, reliving again and again her dumping him. Who did she think she was? She should be grateful he ever laid eyes on her. She would regret this when she would lie alone in bed night after night.

He suddenly stopped walking. Did she lie alone, he wondered? It was not so hard for widows to be 'merry'. In fact, widows were, in a way, in an advantageous position. Compared to married or unmarried women, who were under the dominion of the husband or father, they enjoyed more freedom and could make their own decisions.

He took a piece of *tsamarella* and washed it down with a shot of *zivania*. He took to pacing again. Is that why she turned him down? Why would she encourage him though? Oh, this woman made his blood boil! He poured himself one more shot... and another one... and another.

He summoned Nikeforos, and when he appeared at his door, he ordered him to saddle the horses. "We're going out," Marin announced with resolve.

"*Signore* Jacomo as well?

"No, just you and me."

"Where are we going, Master Marin?"

"To the brothel with the new girls."

---

1 Salted sundried, deboned goat's meat, sprinkled with oregano.

Nikeforos didn't know if he should be relieved or worried. Ever since that snakebite, his master hadn't been himself. He wouldn't go out much, nor did he care for female company. And now he was ready for action again. Nikeforos would have thought that Marin had recovered if it hadn't been for the empty *zivania* bottle on the table.

About an hour later, the two young men tied their horses safely outside the brothel by the castle. Nikeforos went for a stroll at the beach to wait for his master. His Orthodox faith did not allow him to use women like this. He would find a nice girl and marry one day soon, he reminded himself avoiding temptation - hopefully Persephone. She was almost a young woman now. She was close to fourteen. Perhaps it was time he sent the matchmaker to her parents to ask for her hand in marriage. Giving a bride price equal to Persephone's small dowry wouldn't be a problem. Providing a house would. However, Marin had promised to help him if her parents agreed.

In the brothel, a beautiful blonde in a see-through robe came to take Marin by the hand.

"You look like you're carrying the world on your shoulders. Let me give you a bath and a massage with aromatic oils. That should relieve you from the tension," she suggested in a soft, sweet voice, and Marin followed her obediently.

In the tub in her chambers, he closed his eyes concentrating on her touch, but when he opened them again in the reality of the brothel, he found he was irritated. He got out of the water and dried himself up hastily. The girl got out of the tub, too, and put on her see-through robe that stuck on her sensual body.

"Have I not pleased you, *signore*? Tell me what you would like me to do!"

With swift movements, Marin got dressed. "It's got nothing to do with you. You did everything right." He left some money on her dresser and left.

If Nikeforos was surprised his master showed up so soon wearing a somber face, he didn't show it. Should Marin want to confide in him, he knew he would take his secret to his grave.

56

2011

Lorenzo looked at her puzzled. "This is not the way to the hotel, is it?"

"No, it's not." Marina said with a smirk.

"Why do I have this feeling you're up to something?" He gave her a half smile.

"I thought you might want to have dinner like the average Cypriot does," she said, casting a glance in his direction. The five-o'clock shadow on his face gave him a rough charm, she noticed, but she immediately focused her gaze on the road again.

"Anything that has to do with food has my attention."

"We'll just have to make a quick stop. I'll pick up the chronicle," she said, getting into the right hand lane on the coastal road, taking a right and right again into St. Andrews Street. "I'll only by a minute," she said and appeared with a book in her hand only a couple of minutes later. After a very short drive, they parked the car and started walking toward the castle.

Lorenzo admired the illuminated medieval structure with the two-meter thick walls and the cozy old neighborhood. Despite the chilly weather, people were enjoying their drinks at the lined up cafés and restaurants in the pedestrian zone under the heaters on the sidewalks.

"What is this place?" he asked, looking around.

"This is a very popular place with the locals for an evening out. It forms the western part of the old town, and this castle here was built in the 14th century on the site of an earlier Byzantine castle. Its function was to protect the harbor and the town. King Richard married Berengaria here and crowned her Queen of

England and Cyprus. This street was named after them. The castle also houses a medieval museum with relics from the Frankish and the Venetian Periods."

Lorenzo took a look around. "Charming!"

"It's a pity you are staying such a short time. There are so many beautiful places and historical sites we won't be able to visit," Marina said with regret.

"I could always come back – perhaps in the summer time." He gave her an attractive smile.

"You'd love it... Would you rather sit inside or outside? Outside is more beautiful but inside is warmer."

"My guess is you like it warm."

"I'm fine either way," Marina lied unconvincingly.

Lorenzo smiled and shook his head. He pushed the restaurant door, held it open for her, and gallantly placed his palm on her back.

"You come here often?" he asked when they were finally left alone at a quiet corner table. He couldn't help noticing how all the waiters turned to greet her with a nod of the head.

"Uh, if working here counts, then yes. I help out sometimes."

Lorenzo looked at her through half-closed eyes, pondering what a busy little life she led and gave her an affable smile. A waiter came to their table and served a variety of small cold *meze* dishes, and Lorenzo looked up at her in astonishment.

"Have we ordered?"

"*I* did when we came in." A cheeky smirk spread across her face as his brows arched. "Do you trust me?" She used the same conspiratorial tone of voice he used the night before when he undertook ordering.

"I'm sure you can do a much better job ordering Cypriot food than me. Now, I'm curious. You'll have to explain all these little dishes in detail to me."

"First of all, it's essential to understand the concept of *meze*. You see *meze* in Greek means more than satisfying an empty stomach; it's an experience. It's a combination of small quantities of a variety of dishes, enjoyed in good company while drinking, chatting, and laughing."

Marina gladly went on to elaborate on the refined *meze* dishes served.

57

1467

Since his last encounter with Elena, Marin had been suffering from insomnia. She hounded not only his sleep but also his equanimity. The serfs at work and the servants at home tried to stay out of his way and his temper.

Determined to forget all about her, he forced himself to work harder and slogged away at the mill and cotton farm ledgers even longer than usual. He went to bed as late and as exhausted as possible, in the hope that fatigue would grant him his hard-earned sleep.

In spite of the measure of his resolve, he would get out of bed in the dead of the night, light a candle, and in the company of red wine, let his fingers slip along the little wooden cross she had carved for him. Out of the chest, he would take out the drawing of Elena feeding Ioanna and stare at it, playing in his mind the few encounters they had. Upset, he would crinkle and toss it, only to pick it up lovingly later and straighten it.

He endured in agony, waiting for the effect of the love potion to diminish. She must have used a double dose, he assumed, for it had been two weeks, and he was still tormented. What added to his ordeal was Nikeforos's courting Persephone since her parents' consent in marriage. They would soon be setting the date for the engagement.

Meanwhile, Elena knew Marin would come back to her sooner or later. She just had to decide what she wanted when he did.

58

2011

"So you're still a chef at the Intercontinental somewhere?" Marina took one last *loukoumas*[1] and a spoon of ouzo ice cream.

"Not anymore. When Beth died, I had two options. I could either focus on my career or on my daughter. I chose the latter. 'Two roads diverged in a wood, and I – I took the one less traveled by'. Or maybe not."

"'And that has made all the difference'," she finished off the verse. A faint smile crossed their faces, as they locked eyes. "So you're no longer with the hotel?" Marina broke the silence.

"No, I moved to Rovigo. It's a small town. It's better for Paola. Anyway, I opened up my own restaurant, Ca' Lorenzo. It's in the central square next to the City Hall. You should come one day. Ever been?"

Marina cleared her throat and stared at her hands. "I haven't had the chance to travel much yet. You?"

Lorenzo flashed a warm smile at her. "I spent some time in a few parts of the world working for the Intercontinental. Beth and I...," he pressed his lips together as if to take the words back, "… liked experiencing flavors of the world."

"You miss her, don't you?" Marina offered him a congenial smile.

"I'd be lying if I said I didn't. We had a good life together - short but happy. We loved the same things."

Marina looked at him and wondered what she could possibly have in common with him.

"And although I haven't been romantically involved with anyone ever since, I know it's time I moved on with my life," he said, knowing he hadn't done a good job at that yet.

---

1 Honey dumpling.

"It's hard to turn theory into practice, I guess." Marina wondered why he wasn't dating anyone. Surely Italy was overflowing with beautiful women.

"Let's say I haven't found anyone I feel I want to connect with yet." He looked up at her and held her in a vulnerable gaze. "Or maybe I have, but it's been so long since I last flirted that I'm afraid I'm a bit out of practice."

Could he be talking about her? Probably not, she decided. She had a sip of water and changed the subject. "Do you regret moving to Rovigo?"

He looked at her as if he might have expected a different response and then said, "You know, I take my time and think things through before I make a decision that might have an impact on my life or Paola's. Moving to Rovigo was a conscious decision, and no, I don't regret it. Rovigo can put the spell on you with its provincial laid-back lifestyle and friendly neighbors. Of course, it's not the center of the gastronomic world, but I can live with that. I have time for my daughter... And this is also the reason why I'll probably say 'no' to participating at a chef competition at LA9 Sat, a local TV station in Padua, as a judge. It's just a forty-minute drive from Rovigo, but soon Paola will be calling Sofia 'mom' and me 'uncle'." He tried to joke about it.

"I bet you're exaggerating... You know, this could be good promotion for your restaurant. And I can imagine that taking part in a TV show can be fun. Isn't there a way you could involve Paola? Not just the time in the car but also show her a bit of Padua each time? She might even be allowed to watch you from the vicinity in the studio. That would be an exciting experience for her!"

Lorenzo rested his index finger on his temple and contemplated Marina's angle. "You might be right. I should sleep on it perhaps."

59

1467

Marin was pacing up and down in his chamber one sleepless night. He stopped, gulped down his wine, and with a determined move, he took his chemise off, got dressed, hashed the hound dogs at the entrance, and tiptoed out of the tranquil Cornaro mansion. He reached the stables in resolute strides, got on his horse, and headed north.

Elena was awakened by the banging on her door in the middle of the night. She quickly checked on Ioanna who was sound asleep. Only Hippocrates was alert, but Elena silenced him with her motion. She lit the oil lamp on the bedside table, slipped into her slippers, and walked to the door.

"Who's there?" she asked through the closed door.

"Elena, open up. It's Marin." His voice sounded tormented.

"It's the middle of the night!"

"I know. I'm sorry I woke you up, but I have to see you. I have to talk to you."

She put her hand on her hip. "Are you drunk?" she asked distrustfully.

"No... Maybe... A little." He chuckled.

"Can't this wait until the morning?"

"No, it's urgent."

Elena frowned. Against her better judgment, she opened the door, but instead of letting him in, she stepped outside on the moonlit porch. She shivered in the chill of the night. Her erect nipples, evident through her chemise, stared at him demanding his attention, but he commanded all his self-restraint and resisted the impulse to bend down and taste them. That would scare her off. Following his gaze, Elena folded her arms in front of her chest. He swallowed hard and tried to concentrate on her face.

"What do you want, Marin?"

"You!" He fixed his erotic Glaucous blue gaze on her brown eyes.

"What?" She whispered caught off guard. She did not expect such a bold, plain-spoken statement. Nor did she expect it to stir such a yearning for him.

He darted his ardent eyes at her as he took a step closer. Elena could smell the alcohol in his breath, but he couldn't be all that drunk if he rode all the way from the Cornaro mansion in the dead of the night.

"Elena! Oh, Elena! You have taken away my sleep... my peace of mind." He fondled her hair. "I can't stop thinking about you."

Enthralled by the dancing flames of passion in his eyes, Elena watched him lean into her, as he took her face in his two hands and brushed his lips against hers. Unable to struggle against his pheromones, she closed her eyes and let go. Marin gave in to her intoxicating kiss like to good vintage wine that he tasted over and over again. His lips evoked senses that had been dormant for too long for such a young woman.

"Oh, Elena. I have to have you, or I'll die," he whispered in her ear, and his warm breath filled her with thrill. Feeling his urgency to be with her made her own desire flare, as they explored each other hungrily until their breaths eventually became one in the stillness of the night.

60

2011

"I still don't feel comfortable about your getting the dinner bill," Lorenzo said when she put her foot on the brake in the hotel parking lot.

Marina killed the engine and looked at his earnest expression. "I just wanted to return last night's hospitality."

He sighed and took her hand in his and brought it to his lips. "I know. Just let *me* get the bills when we're together. All right?" he asked.

Marina smiled at his old-fashioned, yet cute manners, nodded, and picked up the chronicle from the backseat. A couple of minutes later, they were taking a seat at the bar, and Paul greeted them with a smile.

Lorenzo turned to her and asked "is there anything typically Cypriot you would recommend?"

"A few drinks actually. Would you like to try our national cocktail? Brandy sour?"

"Sure." Lorenzo shrugged, and Paul got to business.

"*Yeia mas*!" Marina raised her glass when Paul placed two cocktail glasses in front of them.

"*Yeia mas*!" Lorenzo matched the toast in Greek and took a reconnaissance sip of his cocktail.

"There's a story behind our brandy sour."

"Why does this not surprise me?" Lorenzo gave her a cheeky smirk, but Marina didn't mind.

"In the thirties, the young King Farouk of Egypt would often visit the Forest Park Hotel in Platres. He had a preference for cocktails, so at the hotel, they developed this cocktail with brandy and lemon squash especially for him but served it as iced tea to disguise the alcohol in it - him being Muslim and all."

"To King Farouk and the barman who came up with the idea!" he said, raising his glass as the pianist sat at the piano and started playing *Sway.*

"Just one dance?" he asked, extending his arm.

"I'm not that much of a dancer." Marina shrugged uncomfortably.

"Just follow my lead," he said, flashing an encouraging smile at her.

He led her to the dance floor and placed his right arm on her left shoulder blade, keeping the right space between them. She timidly placed her left hand on his right shoulder and put her right hand in his that he lifted a bit higher up. He explained the basic one-two-three-four mambo steps, and they began to sway to the rhythm. Feeling her tense in his arms, he bent close to her ear and whispered, "Relax. Just feel the rhythm and let go. The rest comes naturally."

Marina loosened her hips and even her head each time she counted 'two'.

"Much better," he praised her. "Want to try a simple twirl?" he raised the stakes when her steps became more self-confident.

"How do I do that?" she accepted the challenge with a glint in her eyes.

"Just go underneath my arm, twirl, and spin back to me."

He made everything sound so easy, Marina thought, and gave it a try. Her face was ablaze with excitement when the twirl worked, and she spun back into his arms.

Lorenzo rewarded her with a radiant smile. "You're a natural!" He showed her a couple more moves, happy to see her smiling face.

Marina was so into performing the dance steps right that she looked around flabbergasted when the pianist stopped several songs later for his break.

"Wow! That was great, thanks… But I really think it's time we looked at the chronicle."

"Sure. Would you like to go over it in my room? It's quieter there," he said casually.

Marina hesitated for a moment before saying, "I'm sure we can find a quiet corner in the lobby."

Lorenzo stretched his arm for her to lead the way.

61

1467

Marin quickly solved the cryptogram she had left him as a clue and read the decrypted riddle one more time.

Where the tree that gives us the liquid gold and the tree whose leaves Pythia ate at Delphi lean on the tree whose seeds are gauge for jewelers' carat, you'll find me.

He scratched the back of his head. This woman always had a way of adding a touch of extraordinariness to their encounters. He had come up with an extraordinary idea, too, that he couldn't wait to share with her. Provided he found her first, he thought, and chuckled. He had a rough idea where she might be.

He followed the stream up the hill to the spot where an olive tree and a bay leaf tree leaned on a carob tree. He remembered that spot only too well because that's where they last bathed together.

He found her reading aloud Dante's *Divina Commedia*, which he had asked his father to bring from Venice, to Ioanna, who was rolling on the blanket by her side, and to Hippocrates that was dozing off in the heat. Elena was sitting in the shade of the century old tree with her back leaning against its trunk, half-hidden amongst the tall pink and white oleanders. The moment she saw him approach, she sprang to her feet, filled her palms with water from the stream, and when he came to stand close to her, she sprinkled him with water.

"Hey! What was that for?" he asked startled but smiling.

"It's Pentecost today. It's bad luck if you don't get wet." She gave him a glowing smile.

"In that case..."

Marin lifted her up and let her fall in the shallow water of the stream. Elena left out a cry. She decided not to get up, and Marin lent her his arm to help her up, while Ioanna started crawling in their direction curious about this new kind of game. Hippocrates joined them barking and shaking his tail. Elena dragged Marin with all her might - a move he had not anticipated. He lost his balance and fell in the water, too, just as Ioanna took to crawling over them giggling.

Marin burst out laughing. "Does that mean we'll have plenty of good luck?" he asked while helping the women in his life, as he called them, out of the water.

"I'd like to hope so!" Elena said and took Ioanna's clothes off and let them dry on nearby bushes. It was such a sunny day.

Watching over Ioanna, who was still discovering the fallen leaves and the rocks in the stream, Marin asked, "What happens if I can't decipher your riddles and can't find you one day?"

"I knew you'd find me!"

"Yes, but what if I can't?" He looked at her curiously.

"I'll send Hippocrates to your aid, but I don't think this will be necessary. You are too smart."

"And motivated," he said, not hiding how pleased he was with her compliment!

Elena made herself comfortable under the carob tree again, and Marin lay down by her side with Ioanna on his chest and rested his head on her lap. Hippocrates made himself comfortable at their feet.

"Why don't you read to me?" he encouraged her while patting the baby's back.

"No, I'm tired. Reading is more difficult than speaking. I have to read most of it twice to understand it anyway." She caressed his hair and massaged his temples.

"Mm... That's good," he whispered. His rhythmical breathing soon pacified Ioanna who fell asleep.

Elena looked at the serene expression on his handsome face. She had vowed to expect nothing of him, but Marin's frequent visits made it harder and harder. He was careful not to make any promises, although he sometimes teased her that she was his little witch who had bewitched him for eternity.

But what would a bourgeois Venetian want with a common plebeian like herself? Sooner or later, his beloved uncle would find a suitable bride for him. Marriage had always been a means to climb up politically, financially, and socially. Why would Marin be an exception?

Elena decided to live their romance to the fullest for as long as it lasted and make it last for as long as she could. She watched the bond between Marin and her baby daughter grow stronger by the visit and was both content and concerned.

Marin opened his eyes and saw her pensive little face. "A sezin for your thoughts," he said and smiled at her.

Elena couldn't possibly share her thoughts with him. Instead, she chewed on a carob and relaxed her back against the trunk of the tree.

"How would you feel if a mightier nation came to Venice, took your land, your produce, your possessions and made serfs out of you?"

Marin closed his eyes again. He could imagine where this was leading. And it was such a great, lazy afternoon! He sighed. He knew Elena was too much of a free spirit to accept the world as it was. This little non-conformist creature had the strength and the wisdom to slip through the system and live a life by her own rules.

"It's not like serfs are starving," he said with his eyes still closed.

"But they do sometimes. We produce so much grain here in

Cyprus, and it's hardly ever enough to feed us all because you take it!"

"*I* take it?" He opened his eyes.

"Foreigners take it. Foreigners only want us to work harder so that they can profit more. This is our land we are talking about. Our produce! Our lives!"

Marin sat up carefully next to her so as not to wake Ioanna who was resting peacefully in his arms.

"Your land, your produce, your lives belong to your king," he said in a low voice.

"Like yours belong to the doge?"

"Our system is not exactly the same - but yes."

"Only your doge is always Venetian. Our king is always a foreigner. Look at the Venetians' way of life, like you described it to me, and look at our lives!"

"I see what you mean. Look! It's not like we want to make serfs suffer. We need hands to work the fields and the mill. Elena, if we sometimes seem harsh it's because serfs are lazy."

"Lazy? Give them back their freedom, their pride, and pay them for their work, and they won't be lazy."

"We couldn't possibly do that. There would be no profit left."

"Less profit you mean... But surely, you can treat them like human beings. They are not different than you or me!"

"Come on, Elena. They are a bunch of ignorant peasants."

"Of course, they are ignorant. What chance do they have at literacy?"

"What do you want me to do, Elena? I can't change the system. I can't set them free. They don't even belong to me."

"Maybe not. But there is no excuse not to treat them with dignity."

"That I could perhaps work on," he said, seeking reconciliation.

She rested her head on his shoulder. "Wouldn't it be great if all people could be masters of their own destiny? Free to choose where to live, whom to marry. Free to work their own land – have a right at literacy."

Marin wondered how the Cornaro enterprises would survive in a world like that but refrained from voicing his thoughts. *It is easy to accept living in a world of injustice when you are favored*, he thought.

When he had sailed from Venice that cold rainy January morning, he didn't expect to find a woman so fascinating in the middle of nowhere. There was just one thing he could not explain even to himself. Why did he conceal his father's and brothers' visits from Elena and why did he avoid mentioning Elena when his father asked if there was a woman in his life?

"I've brought backgammon and chess. Choose your game, *signore!*" Elena said to lighten up the conversation.

"Let's play backgammon now. We can play chess at home. I've an idea how we could raise the stakes and make it more... interesting."

Elena raised an inquisitive eyebrow.

"Strip chess!" he said and smiled mischievously. "I'll explain later."

62

2011

Lorenzo looked up from the screen and found he was filled with the same excitement as before when he was holding her in his arms on the dance floor. With a smirk on his face, he observed her alert eyes scanning the book for reference to his ancestor.

At first, Marina had made an effort to translate the chronicle to him, but it soon became obvious how time consuming this exercise was. Instead, they decided she should go about browsing the chronicle while Lorenzo would search for Zanettis in Cyprus online.

Feeling someone staring at her, Marina cast a cursory glance around until her eyes rested on his familiar smiling face. "Any luck?" she asked.

"Well, there seem to be a few Zanettis here, but I've no way of telling whether they are related to my ancestor or not. You?"

"No, nothing yet. Unfortunately, I can't read quite as fast as I would like. This mixture of medieval Cypriot Greek combined with all these Frankish administrative terms takes more time than I had expected... Anyway, it's late. I think I should be going now. I'll try and finish this at home."

"Sure."

Lorenzo got up to walk her to her car, aware that he hadn't spent such an enjoyable day for a long time. They reached the parking lot in a leisurely pace, and Marina opened the door to the driver's seat. She looked over her shoulder to wish him 'goodnight' but found herself unprepared for the proximity of his body and his mesmerizing gaze. Slowly, he bent down and bashfully put his lips on hers.

"I shouldn't," Marina whispered.

"Shouldn't?" he echoed her words.

Her mouth suddenly felt dry. "Well, you are a client."

"I was hoping you saw more than just a client in me," he said with a shy smile.

Marina lowered her gaze, and he removed a curl from her eye. He put his arm around her slim waist, and she made no effort to stop him. He kissed her on the forehead and brushed his cheek against hers. She felt his warm breath as the corners of their mouths touched, and her lips parted.

She thought she heard the sound of violins but realized it was just his ringtone when he sighed and took his cell phone out of his pocket.

"I miss you, too, angel. Can I call you back?" she heard him say tenderly in Italian.

Marina swiftly sat behind the wheel, wondering what on earth had gotten into her flirting like that with a client. It was unprofessional – unacceptable.

Lorenzo bent his knees while holding onto the door. "Marina, I only answered the phone to say I'll call back later!"

"Yeah, well... Look, it's late. Same time tomorrow?"

And then it hit him that she understood Italian.

"Marina!" He put his finger under her chin and gently turned her face to him. "Are you running away from me?"

She cast her gaze to her hands on the steering wheel and remained silent.

"Don't... That was Paola on the phone," he said gently.

Marina studied his face and said quietly, "It really is late. I have to go. Goodnight." She shifted into reverse and pulled out of the parking lot.

63

1468

Marin was on his way to the stables to ride out to yet another clandestine nocturnal encounter with Elena.

"Master Marin!" Nikeforos managed to catch up with him just as Marin was about to get into his saddle.

He spun around feeling like a burglar. "What is it, Nikeforos?" he asked, thinking this couldn't be good.

"Master Cornaro has just arrived from Nicosia and is waiting for you in his office," Nikeforos said slightly out of breath still.

Marin nodded and gave Nikeforos the reins of his horse.

"Master Marin, beware of Jacomo," Nikeforos warned him. "He pretends to be your friend, but I think he's a snitch. He was talking about you when your uncle summoned me, but he stopped as soon as he saw me. And I didn't like the look on his face."

"Thank you, Nikeforos," Marin said and went back into the mansion.

In these last few days, he thought Jacomo's eyes were fixed on him. He wondered what he might have told Andrea. The work at the mill was as usual. What did he have on him, he wondered?

"You have asked to see me, uncle," Marin said when he joined Andrea in the library.

"Uh, there you are, my boy. Yes, I'd like to discuss certain issues with you. I have asked the servants not to disturb us until dinner is ready." He beckoned to Marin to take a seat.

Marin tried to hide his uneasiness. Discourse with Andrea was usually lengthy. He could guess there would be no seeing Elena tonight. He just wished there was some way to notify her. He had been very careful not to let anyone know about her, except for his trusted friend Nikeforos, although his frequent ride outs did not go unnoticed. Is that what Jacomo told Andrea?

He tried hard to concentrate on what his uncle was saying to him about the latest developments in the palace. Marin's attention span was noticeably shorter than usual that evening. Only when Andrea asked him about their enterprises, did he seem to be fully alert.

They had a brief break when they moved to the dining room where dinner was served. When the last servant left, Andrea chewed up his bite of *tavas*[1] and said, "I'd like you to come with me to Nicosia tomorrow. There's this banquet at the palace gardens, and I think it's time I introduced you to the bourgeoisie and some of the nobility here. I should have done that earlier," he said, almost talking to himself. *Only I hadn't expected you to fall in love so soon*, he thought.

Marin figured it could take days to be introduced even to some of the three hundred nobles and knights, two hundred squires and numerous bourgeois families on the island, but he forced a smile on his face and said, "thank you, uncle."

---

1 Goat meat, baked with onions in red wine and mixed spices.

64

2011

When Lorenzo woke up the next morning, his first thoughts were of Marina. His yawn turned into a grin as he considered her schoolgirl nervousness when he tried to kiss her the night before. He got out of bed, undressed for the shower, and hurried down to meet her.

At breakfast that morning, Marina was less gregarious than usual. Lorenzo observed how the constant buzzing of her cell irritated her, and how she chose to push the ignore button.

"You could take your calls," he encouraged her.

"This is a call I'd rather not take right now," she murmured and took a sip of her coffee absent-mindedly, looking at the bouncy reflection of the sunbeams on the water through the large French windows.

"Your mom finally gave in?" he asked casually, as he helped himself to a cinnamon roll.

Marina looked up at him startled. For a moment, she had forgotten how easy it had been to open up to him. She nodded and put her cell phone on silent mode, angry at George for not leaving her mother alone.

"He's quite persistent," Lorenzo noticed.

"You can say that again." The corners of her mouth twitched.

"You don't forgive easily, do you?" He studied her expressive face.

"That's not it. I just have nothing else to say to him," she said a bit more emphatically than she intended.

"I don't suppose you had the time to browse through the chronicle last night," Lorenzo calmly changed the subject.

"Actually, I did, but I'm afraid I'm not any wiser. There are several references to Venetians but none to Marin Zanetti per se - or any other Zanetti for that matter. I'm sorry... I've prepared an itinerary for today. Would you like to see it?" She passed him the folder she took out of her bag.

"I have full faith in you. Surprise me," he said and offered her a warm smile.

65

1468

Andrea Cornaro didn't need to show his invitation at the palace gates. The guards recognized him at once and made way for them to pass. Marin looked right and left, dazzled at the gathered royalty and aristocracy dressed up in exquisite colorful garments in the magnificence of the illuminated imperial gardens. The Auditor of the Kingdom and his protégé mingled amongst the guests to the sound of the palace musicians that warm mid-summer evening, so that Andrea could introduce Marin to some of the important noble and bourgeois families on the island, like the Viscontis, the Querinins, the Donatos, the Loredanos, and the Pessaros.

The *Consigliere* had arranged for Marin to sit next to Anna Contarini, the niece of Zorzi Contarini, a rich Venetian merchant dealing with lace and fabrics. Anna was an enrapturing blonde, blue-eyed beauty, educated, swank, with refined manners. She had just arrived from Venice, fully informed of the latest gossip, and took to flirting with Marin at once. Flattered with the attention he received and perhaps a bit out of practice ever since he had met Elena, Marin was unprepared for this siren that had come to the banquet with the sole mission of weaving a seductive web around him.

Marin glanced around at the sumptuous extravagance of the palace, the ample food and good wine, and the high spirits of the banquet when he heard Zorzi Contarini invite them to dinner the next day. Andrea accepted the invitation graciously, and Marin wasn't sure he liked the satisfied look on the two men's faces.

Anna turned to him and offered him a self-confident, shining smile, her conquering smile that revealed her alabaster teeth and the dimples under her high cheekbones, and asked Marin to dance with her. Anna wasn't sure she fully agreed with her uncle's choice. Deep down she was convinced she could do better than a mill supervisor, even if he was Cornaro's protégé. She decided to play along, however, until she could have a better understanding of the nobility on the island. As long as she was not married to the boy, she would be watchful for someone with a title and more money. At least, he was handsome, she thought.

Marin escorted her to the dance floor and held her voluptuous figure in his hands dance after dance, trying to decide what Andrea was up to.

66

2011

The car went up the winding mountain road before it came to a halt at the ruins of a fourteenth century stone-built monastery.

"Where are we?" Lorenzo asked, getting out of the car.

"This is one of my favorite villages, Anogyra. It used to be the regional center for the carob trade. The caravans of camels and donkeys used to head down to the jetty at Avdimou, carrying panniers laden with carobs for export. Carob was so important for the island's economy that it was called Cyprus' black gold. This tiny chapel and these ruins here are what remain of the Monastery of the Holy Cross. According to a local legend, St. Elena left a piece of the wood of the Holy Cross here on her way back from the Holy Land, although this is highly unlikely."

The old wooden door creaked as she pushed it open. Lorenzo looked up at the remnants of the fifteenth-century frescoes on the ceiling, probably drawn by monks who fled the fall of Constantinople.

"I'm not much of a churchgoer, but this is serene."

"Don't worry. We did not come to Anogyra on a pilgrimage."

In the dim light of the small chapel, he watched her leave a coin in a tray, light a candle, walk to the icon of Jesus first, make the sign of the cross – three fingers, right to left - and kiss the icon. She repeated the same ritual with the few other icons before she met him again at the entrance. Her face was much calmer, he noticed.

"You're sure we did not come here on a pilgrimage? I could swear I heard you praying for the twenty-first," he teased her as they were walking away from the chapel.

"That too... Ever since I've found out about this place, I come up here whenever something is bothering me," she replied, and Lorenzo wondered what could possibly be bothering her. "Our trip today is more of a culinary discovery though." Marina put on her professional expression again.

"Culinary sounds already a lot more interesting," Lorenzo said and took a photo of her with the ruins as background.

"Maybe I should take some photos of you," Marina suggested and Lorenzo put the camera in her hand.

Marina did her best to use her imagination for more artistic snapshots. "I hope, at least, some of them are good," she said a few minutes later when she gave him back the camera, and they set off.

The car stopped its ascent toward the little village of not more than two hundred and fifty inhabitants, so a flock of goats could go by. The shepherd, riding his donkey languidly, raised his hand to greet them, and Marina and Lorenzo waved back at him.

"Wow! Beautiful!" Lorenzo cried out excitedly hidden behind the camera.

"This is authentic Cyprus," Marina said, waiting patiently for the goats to cross the road before she continued to drive toward the village for a mile or so up the winding country lane.

67

1468

Agony took the place of the euphoria her relationship with Marin had filled her with, and Elena became self-critical for having let her guard down. He came into her life and splashed joyful colors on the grey canvas of her monotonous existence. And now? Not knowing what had happened was more painful than she could bear. She gradually began to appreciate the magnitude of her mother's drama.

She had a bad feeling about his lengthy absence, but she kept telling herself there had to be an explanation for it. From what she had been able to find out from women's gossip in the village, he had ridden with his uncle to Nicosia to be introduced to other Venetian families. Elena knew she had no claim on him and that one day she would lose him. She feared that this day had come.

In the meantime in Nicosia, one invitation followed another, as bourgeois families were only too eager to entertain the Kingdom's Auditor and his protégé. If it was a coincidence that the Contarini were always invited, too, Marin wasn't sure, but he feared he could now see through Andrea's plan.

When Marin mentioned he should be getting back to the mill and the estates, Andrea found all sorts of excuses to prolong his stay in the cosmopolitan capital. The young Venetian felt little surprise when later that evening, Andrea discussed an engagement to the Contarini girl.

"Don't be concerned with the bride price, Marin. You know you've always been like a son to me. *I* will match Anna's dowry and provide the house. Consider this as my wedding gift to you. Soon, you will be able to start up your own business," Andrea said while they were enjoying a *commandaria* after dinner.

Marin contemplated the size of the fortune that would be bestowed on him with awe. A million things he could accomplish with so much money. His racing mind was already exploring all the possibilities. He could have everything but Elena, he thought. Andrea didn't fail to notice the corners of the young man's mouth twitch.

"That doesn't mean you can't see that native anymore – discreetly, of course," Andrea said as if reading the young man's mind.

Marin pursed his lips. He felt little surprise that Andrea was so well-informed about everything.

"Anna Contarini is your perfect match, Marin. Believe me, I considered all available options. It would mean a lot to me to see you married into this family. Now, I know that your mind is set on that widow, but when you give yourself some time to consider your good fortune with Anna, I'm sure you'll thank me for this."

Marin looked at him silently, cast his gaze on his glass, and downed his *commandaria*.

68

2011

In Anogyra, Lorenzo watched the demonstration of *pastelli*[1]. When he was offered a tasting, he chewed it carefully, trying to decide what was so familiar about the taste.

"You know, this reminds me a lot of the *Elah* toffees we have in Italy," he said while still savoring it. The similarities and the differences in the products and recipes used around the Mediterranean basin always fascinated him.

When Marina took him to the dairy farm to watch a demonstration of freshly made *anari*, he found the likeness to Italian ricotta cheese remarkable. His curiosity to use *halloumi* in a recipe was triggered when he found out that it's the only cheese in the world that can be grilled without melting.

"This tastes really good. Here, try it!" He offered her his plate to taste.

"It's good. I know," Marina said without taking the plate.

"Have some," he insisted, and when she did, he took another picture of her.

"I think you are taking more photos of me than of Cyprus," she said half seriously and half teasingly.

"I know." He lowered his camera and fixed his gaze on her. "You are Cyprus to me - warm and friendly... interesting... beautiful," he said quietly.

Marina cleared her throat. "Speaking of beautiful, we should take a walk in the center of the village. Come on. Let's go. You have to see this."

---

1 Carob toffee.

They thanked the proprietor and walked to the cobbled village square with the quaint stone-built houses and the overhanging wooden balconies adorned with colorful bougainvilleas. Endless hues of geraniums and roses in terracotta pots along the cobbled lanes added an aesthetic final touch to the scenic square.

Outside a little coffee shop, Marina stopped for a moment and cast a glance around, trying to orient herself. The village barber, an elderly man with a warm, friendly smile stepped out of the coffee shop, greeted them, and held a conversation in Greek with Marina. Lorenzo figured he was giving them directions. When several minutes later the elderly man waved at them goodbye, they turned right, followed a narrow lane that passed by the old water spring and reached the winery gate.

"These were long directions for such a short walk," Lorenzo observed.

"He did not just give us directions. He invited us for coffee. Three times," she explained with a smile.

"But he didn't seem to know you, did he?" Lorenzo asked with interest.

"No, we are complete strangers. This is what I love about Cyprus, its people, especially in the villages."

"I'm impressed," he said as the vintner came to greet them and perform a wine tasting for them.

The tour of Anogyra ended with a visit to the olive park where they watched the process of olive oil extraction. They had a *katsoura*[2], watched a short video on the story of olive oil in Cyprus, and walked in the theme park featuring extraction methods of the past and exhibits on how olive oil was used in the Mediterranean diet, in medicine, and for beauty.

When some time later, Lorenzo placed his purchases on the

---

2 Toasted bread with fresh olive oil, sprinkled with oregano.

backseat, he said, "At this rate, I might need to buy one more suitcase."

"You could have a Cyprus night with all this artisanal products when you are back in Rovigo," Marina suggested with a smile as she was opening the driver's door.

"I'd love that," Lorenzo said and sat in the car. He fastened his seat belt and turned and faced her. "Marina, you are a mind reader. I absolutely enjoyed this little village, Ano… What was it called again?"

"Anogyra," Marina said, smiling and drove up the mountain road. The soft Greek 'g' is sometimes difficult for foreigners to pronounce.

"Where are we going now?" Lorenzo took a look at the scenery.

"I thought you wanted this to be a surprise," Marina teased him.

"Touché… What a beautiful day! Nothing like the storm when I arrived on Monday."

"It's the halcyon days."

"Nice!" he said, stretching his right arm and casually letting it rest on the back of her seat.

69

1468

Elena adjusted her headdress properly, made the sign of the cross, and entered the chapel. She left a *gros petit* in the tray, lit a candle, and walked to the icon of Jesus Christ. She made the sign of the cross, said a short prayer, and kissed the icon. When she had repeated the same procedure with the other icons, she cast a glance in awe at the *Pantocrator* of the dome extending his right hand in blessing and prayed one last time.

An old monk leaned on the entrance door for a moment to catch his breath and dragged his old feet toward the *analogion*[1]. His ability to walk was diminishing fast with each passing day.

"Thank you for seeing me, Father Efrem." Elena kissed the hand of her *starets*[2], and he kindly patted her head.

"Come, my dear child. You have come from afar to see an old monk like me." He placed the Gospel Book and a blessing cross on the *analogion* and read an admonition warning for a full confession, holding nothing back.

"Father Efrem, I'm afraid I've committed the same sin as my mother and my nana before me."

Father Efrem, who had been the family confessor starting from her grandfather, looked at her with sincere sympathy without judging. "Giving life is not a sin; taking it is... Is this new life a love child?"

Elena nodded.

"Child, you are not here just to hear the Prayer of Absolution. What torments you so?"

---

1 The lectern.

2 Her spiritual father.

"I hear he's to get engaged to someone else."

"Rumors are not always accurate. Have you talked to him?"

"I can't. He's been in Nicosia for days now... I'm afraid this time rumors are true... He's Venetian. And he's getting engaged to one of his own." She pursed her lips.

"Child, have I ever told you the story about the Christian who wanted to exchange the cross God gave him to carry with another?"

Elena shook her head negatively.

"God gives us all a cross to carry. This symbolizes the difficulties we face here on earth. Well, there was this Christian who complained to God that the cross He had given him was too uncomfortable for him and asked if he might be permitted to exchange it for another. The good Lord lent him a sympathetic ear and showed him where the warehouse with the crosses was. The Christian put his cross down and tried carrying the crosses in the warehouse one by one. When the day was done, he said to God, 'Thank You, Lord, for the opportunity to exchange my cross with another. This one is by far the most convenient to carry.' And then God replied, 'Child, this is the cross you have brought back.'... The Lord never gives us more weight to carry than we can actually bear. We should not despair. Faith! This is our strength."

"I'm just worried about what will become of my children if anything happens to me."

"Child, the Lord provides for all his children, but He also acts in mysterious ways. His plan for our lives is like a piece of embroidery. Only He can see the beautiful side with the design from above. Down here, we can only see the back side with the knots and the threads hanging, and we are unable to comprehend the majestic work of art He has designed for us."

70

2011

The car came to a halt at the parking lot close to the stone-paved Omodhos bustling square with the whitewashed and stone-built houses, the mulberry trees, the tavernas, the coffee shops, and souvenir shops.

"Another monastery!" Lorenzo said, looking at the monastery at the far end of the square.

"Cyprus is sometimes called the island of the saints. In fact, Cyprus was the first Roman province converted to Christianity by Apostle Paul himself. This here is the Monastery of the Holy Cross, famous for its miracles. We can go there later if you like. We can also visit the old wine press and see some beautiful old houses and artisans, but first I've a surprise for you." She looked at him with eyes glistening with excitement, like a child before opening a Christmas gift, and Lorenzo couldn't help grinning.

"Let me guess. It's got to do with food, right?"

"Right! But what?"

"I don't know. A nice lunch somewhere in the village?"

"Close," Marina said and walked to a nearby gate and pushed it open.

"Close?" He asked following her.

"You'll see." Marina knocked on the door and a large woman in her early fifties appeared at the door.

"Uh, Marina! *Kalos Orisate*! Welcome! We've been expecting you. Everything's ready. Come in! Come in!" The large woman gave Marina a warm, squeezing hug.

"Lorenzo, this is Christina. She owns one of the tavernas here in the village, and today she's going to cook just for us, and you're going to cook with her – that is if you like."

"Sure," he said, nodding and smiling.

"Christina will be sharing her kitchen secrets with you."

"Great!" Lorenzo turned to the large woman and shook her hand. "Hello, Christina. What are we cooking today?"

"Hare stew in wine sauce à la Christina. It's a traditional dish, but I've made some slight alterations."

71

1468

As the days succeeded one another without a word from Marin, Elena became conscious of the urgency for pragmatic action. She gazed at the stars above, the spectators of human agony and hope since the creation of the human race and prayed for strength.

She commanded every morsel of her self-discipline and reached the decision to cut the Gordian knot. In her condition, she undertook the Herculean task of gathering livestock and paraphernalia, find lodging by the Catacombs in Paphos, and start afresh. She didn't want to risk going back to Limassol in the vicinity of Ioanna's grandparents. Nor did she think it wise to have her child all alone. She had witnessed too many deaths for that.

Word in the village was that Andrea Cornaro had found a bride for the young master. Elena pondered on her options and decided she would rather not have him at all than share him with his wife. She also decided not to follow in her mother's footsteps. She had Ioanna and her unborn child to care for. She wanted to live for them. Oh, how she wanted to drink from Lethe and erase his memory once and for all! But she couldn't well do that in their love nest, as he called her house.

She wanted to blend into the anonymity of a new place. At least, with the two hundred sezins, she wouldn't have to worry about money for a while. She would settle down and ponder what she should best do with her life. Probably go on with healing – cautiously.

She was heading west, making slow progress on the way to Pafos, when a horseman rode up the hill toward her mud-brick house. The horse followed the familiar route to her place while his master was torn in two inside. He was inflamed with desire to be with her again after so long, yet he knew he should break the news to her.

He wondered sullenly if people really died of broken hearts. He feared that announcing his engagement would open Pandora's Box and tried not to think of the possibility that Elena might harm herself. What would happen to Ioanna? He couldn't live with that. Should he perhaps say nothing and let her love for him fade slowly? What a dilemma! Caught between Scylla and Charybdis, he debated with his inner voice, and prayed to Calliope for eloquent inspiration when he would soon speak to her again.

In front of the porch, Marin pulled the reins and got down. What was that piece of paper hanging on her house door, he wondered? With a swift movement, he took it down. It read, 'farewell, my love. I wish you well.'

"What on earth?" he asked out loud. He tried the door, but it was locked and the windows sealed. The place seemed deserted. He went around the house. Her few animals were gone. "She just took off? Just like that? Without a word?" Marin realized he was talking to himself and tried to snap out of it.

Where did she go? A part of him wanted to get on his horse, search for her, and demand an explanation. Another part told him he was lucky - more than he deserved. Now, he could get engaged to Anna with a light conscious. He just couldn't have Elena any more. He pursed his lips and kicked a broken twig in front of his feet.

72

2011

"What a woman! So friendly - and a great cook!" Lorenzo said grinning, as they left Omodhos behind, ascending further high up.

Marina snorted. "She's had a lot of practice."

"Uh, yes, the tavern."

"That and seven children."

"Seven? Wow! It can never be boring having such a large family," he said.

"Or quiet."

"Don't you like children or are you too young for that?" Lorenzo found himself asking.

"Uh... Yes, I do, and I don't know. I haven't really thought about it yet. I mean I'm not even in a relationship right now. I don't have a real job. But I would like to have children... one day." She locked eyes with him but was unable to make out his thoughts.

She focused her gaze on the road again. A couple of minutes later, she got onto a loose surface road and descended the winding narrow road for a kilometer and a half before she hit the brakes.

"Where are we now?" Lorenzo asked, looking around when he got out of the car.

"We are at the Millomeri waterfalls near Platres," Marina explained as they took to walking. "Platres used to be a feud during the Lusignan Rule. Just above the village, there used to be a Frank Monastery, and its monks were dressed in white, 'platres' in French, hence the name of the village, at least, according to one explanation... Hear the sound of the waterfall?"

Lorenzo strained his ears and nodded. They took to climbing down the steps to the wooden bridge, and the splashing sound of the water got louder and louder until the waterfalls were finally revealed to them. It was a secluded semi circle with the grey stone of the Troodos Mountain, water falling from the top right side from a height of less than twelve meters.

Lorenzo took his camera and started taking pictures of her with the waterfalls as background. "It's small, but it's cute," he said, admiring its unpretentious beauty.

"Further up, in Platres, there's a nice green trek that leads to Kallidonia waterfalls – much bigger and more impressive than this - but it will be dark in a while, so I thought this should do. Besides, this is my favorite. It kind of takes me back through time."

For a while, they just marveled at the natural beauty of the scenery, untouched by human hand, in silence. "We should be getting back. The sun is setting already," Marina remarked.

Lorenzo nodded his consent, and she turned on her feet but slipped on a wet rounded stone and would have landed on all fours if it hadn't been for his quick reflex and strong arms. She locked eyes with him, taken aback by how comfortable it felt in the safety of his arms.

"Thanks," she whispered with an embarrassed smile.

"You're okay?" he asked, gently holding her still.

"Yeah, yeah. I'm fine," she nodded.

Lorenzo gave her a warm smile and casually took her hand in his, and they started making their way back to the car with their hands laced.

73

1468

Elena sighed and lifted Ioanna out of the water. She would have loved to swim again – with him preferably. A couple of fishermen's boats were returning to the safety of the wharf, as she unfolded the blanket on the beach opposite the water castle that the Lusignans had to rebuild after its destruction by an earthquake and a tsunami in 1222 that brought the entire town to its knees.

She sat down with Ioanna and gave her the shells they had collected earlier on their stroll to play with, making sure she wouldn't put them in her mouth. Elena took her pointed knife and started carving the soft piece of wood she found lying on the beach while singing to Ioanna who tried to follow her lead by making incomprehensible sounds.

When Ioanna became disinterested in their duet, Elena let her gaze wander towards the horizon, brooding over how history repeats itself and wondered if the women in her family had been cursed to find a love so heated yet so ephemeral. Twice she had been blessed with a child. Twice she had been left alone with the upbringing of her children. So be it if that was His will. Her only consolation was in prayer. She was certain that the Lord, in His infinite wisdom, had planned a wonderful life for her. She prayed for strength and for enlightenment, for she was, at this stage, unable yet to comprehend His plan for her, or His majestic embroidery design, as Father Efrem had put it. She prayed that God would break this vicious circle and spare her baby the pain.

Ioanna stretched her little arms, and Elena lifted her and rocked her to sleep. The symphony of the murmuring leaves and the burbling waves, licking the shore in front of her bare feet, echoed the whisper of her voice as she said his name time and time again. If only the wind could carry her whisper on its wings to him...

74

2011

"No, a snack is not what I had in mind for tonight. Tonight calls for celebration," Lorenzo said with a touch of mystery, as they were getting into the hotel.

"Why? What's tonight?" Marina smiled, wondering what he might have thought of this time.

"My birthday," Lorenzo said, crossing his fingers behind his back.

"It's your birthday today?" Marina asked for confirmation.

He nodded – his fingers still crossed behind his back.

"Happy birthday!" She gave him a hug and kissed him on both cheeks.

Lorenzo held her in an unfathomable gaze. "Thank you... You know the drill." He pressed the key in her hand.

Marina took it without ado this time and walked to the elevator. When she got into the room, an elegant long white open back dress was laid out on the bed and a pair of matching white shoes on the thick carpet was waiting for her. He had even guessed her size right. Her first reaction was to ignore the dress all together, but then her female vanity dictated that she should at least try it on.

Her lips parted with excitement as she looked at herself in the mirror. Its full length made her look taller and slender. It was a ladylike yet sexy dress, and she instantly fell in love with it.

At the bar, Lorenzo looked up absent-mindedly at her direction, cast his gaze to his drink as if not recognizing her at once, and then swiftly glanced up again to meet her gaze. He gasped. Heads turned around as she walked toward him in her recently-developed *femme fatale* catwalk.

Instinctively, he straightened the collar of his shirt. He rose to his feet, stretched both arms, and said in admiration, "*Che bella!* You look like a Greek goddess. Like Aphrodite."

"Thank you. You shouldn't have," she said all lit up like a Christmas tree.

He let his gaze glide slowly on her from her hair worn up, that gave her a touch of maturity, to her twinkling eyes and inviting smile to her elongated neck and deep décolleté. *She's not wearing a bra*, he thought with a grin, noticing her small, young, firm, rounded breasts. The dress clinched on her slim waist and fell charmingly on her hips and well-shaped legs.

He tilted his head to the side, flared his nostrils, and parted his lips. "My pleasure. I couldn't have you feel underdressed each time we dine together, especially tonight... Turn around. Let me see you."

Marina did, and his gaze was magnetized by the olive skin of her back, the rhythmical movement of her hips and her catwalk. He didn't think much when he was buying her the dress that morning, but he now realized that this was the first time he was allowed a glimpse at her bare skin other than on her face and hands. Feeling his heart pumping faster, he smirked at himself. It was revitalizing to know that he could still feel that way.

"Wow! I'm speechless." He brought his right palm to his heart.

Beaming, Marina took a seat at the bar, placed one leg over the other and a hand on her thigh.

"I hate to leave you alone at the bar, but I need to go and change." He found himself unwilling to tear his gaze away.

"Sure." Marina found the touch of nervousness in his manner sweet and amusing.

Lorenzo waved to the bartender to come closer. "Paul, take care of her for me, will you?" Paul smiled back meaningfully yet tactfully.

"Take care of me?" Marina asked in a low voice.

Casually, Lorenzo let his palm gently brush against the soft skin of her bare back, and whispered in her ear, "There's a reason for everything. I'll explain later." He held her in an intense gaze and gave her an assured half smile. He then straightened his body and picked up the card key she had left for him on the bar. "I'll be right back."

For the first time in a long time, Marina felt that everything was the way it should be, and her grin reached her ears. She kept him in her line of vision for as long as she could and then turned to Paul. "Hi, Paul. Could I have…?"

"A dry martini?" Paul asked while placing the drink in front of her.

Marina flashed a smile at him. "Thank you, Paul. You're a mind reader."

"It comes with the profession." He smiled back and turned to serve the gorgeous, tall blonde who had just walked in through the sliding door and asked if the seat next to Marina was taken.

75

1468

Marin tore his gaze away from the lush décor of *Conte* Visconti's ball-room and caught a glimpse of the secret glances and smiles between the *conte* and Anna, right before their host gathered his courage and approached them to ask Marin for permission to dance a *bassadanza*[1] by Antonio Cornazano with his fiancé. Courteously, Marin nodded his consensus and took note of the *conte's* glowing face.

Despite being short and plump, the *conte* was a smooth dancer. So smooth that no one noticed his swaying away onto the balcony with Anna – no one but Marin. For a moment, he wondered whether he should make a scene but decided against it. Not only had he no desire to insult a powerful man, such as his host, but it suddenly struck him that the *conte's* veiled amorous advances to Anna were an ace up in his sleeve that he shouldn't rush to burn.

With his head filled with memories of his teaching Elena how to dance the *piva*[2] and the *salterello*[3] she enjoyed so much and still incensed about her vanishing into thin air, Marin took his goblet of wine and stepped outside. He sat on a bench in the flower-filled grounds that surrounded the *conte's* mansion, lifted his gaze to the starry sky, and sighed. The engagement was just a few days away, and he had this itch to get onto a galley and go back to Venice. He realized now he never should have agreed to it. Especially now that Anna's true colors were revealed to him, he felt trapped and missed Elena and Ioanna more with each passing day.

---

1 A slow, stately, elegant dance, which accentuates partner interaction and can sometimes be considered processional.

2 A fast, fifteenth century Italian dance.

3 A fast, fifteenth century Italian dance.

Only his word as a gentleman and the fear of displeasing Andrea Cornaro held him from breaking the engagement. He thought about discussing this with his uncle, but he was so burdened with ensuring that the king's engagement to Caterina would prevail despite all his adversaries and their intrigues that he didn't want to disturb him.

Even Nikeforos had discreetly distanced himself ever since Anna came for a visit to the Cornaro mansion. When Marin had once suggested they should celebrate both engagements on the same day, Nikeforos's face was first lit up and then detached. Although he never voiced his thoughts, Marin was certain Nikeforos found dumping Elena unethical. Little did he know that *she* had left him – technically.

Since her disappearance, Marin tried to will Elena out of his conscious mind, but he would now and again yield to the temptation and take the sketches of her and Ioanna out of their hiding place and tenderly let his fingertips slide on their hair and on their cheeks. He knew he had no claim on her. Still, it bothered him that she had written him off just like that.

Yet his own deeds did not exactly honor him either, he thought disapprovingly, and gulped down his wine. He needed to understand why she had left him. He had been half expecting her to beg him to stay. That might have tipped off the balance. But, of course, he couldn't blame her for his actions or inactions.

The young Venetian fixed his stare on the constellation of Ursa Major, the familiar pointer to the north that reminded him of his nights on board. If only he could talk to his parents. The captain would probably tell him to use his brain and study the ramifications of each alternative in depth before making a decision. Marin snorted contemplating what his mother's advice would be, probably "Follow your heart!" The problem was his brain dictated one thing and his heart another.

76

2011

"Barbara?"

Marina turned at the sound of Lorenzo's voice and saw his astonished stare fixed on the gorgeous blonde sitting next to her at the bar.

"Lorenzo, what a coincidence! Isn't this a small world? What are you doing here?" Barbara arched her brows and widened her eyes playfully.

I bet coincidence goes by the name of Sofia, Lorenzo thought and said, "Same as you I guess. Taking a few days off."

Marina looked at clean-shaven, elegant and poised Lorenzo in his classic black Armani suit with subtle stripes, a three-button jacket, and a white shirt. She then looked at the ravishing tall blonde with the very feminine Cavalli black strapless fitted mini dress and out the window went her newly-found female self-assuredness. *She is his surprise birthday gift*, she thought with a tart taste in her mouth.

Marina caught Paul's interested yet discreet stare with the corner of her eye and knew that in the interest of self-preservation, it was time to make an exit. Besides, Lorenzo hadn't addressed a single word to her yet. She inferred that the two had a history together. Her professional duty dictated that she save the day.

She cleared her throat attracting their attention. "Mr. Zanetti, I think here's where I wish you goodnight. Shall I pick you up at ten tomorrow?" Marina asked with the friendliest and most professional smile in her arsenal, figuring that he would be having breakfast with the blonde; therefore, it was not necessary to show up earlier for breakfast.

Lorenzo looked at her and his lips parted like he wanted to say something, but Barbara was faster.

"You have a private guide! Now, that's a bonus to add to your holidays," Barbara said teasingly, looking at Marina from head to toes, but coming from her lips, it sounded almost like an insult.

Lorenzo made the introductions in English, and Marina shook hands with her. "Well, you have to excuse me now. Goodnight," Marina said and forced a smile on her face.

"Let me walk you to your car," Lorenzo offered, but Marina saw Barbara's cheeks stiffen.

"No, no. It's fine. I'm sure you have a lot of catching up to do. I can see myself out. I'll see you in the morning. It was a pleasure, Ms. Bruni."

Marina walked away keeping a stiff upper lip.

77

1468

Marin and Anna were riding side by side northward of the
Cornaro estate. She had asked him to go for a ride in the woods
for their Sunday afternoon ride. He didn't know why subcon-
sciously he brought Anna to Elena's land.

"Is this still part of the Cornaro estates?" Anna asked, looking
around and trying to make conversation.

She couldn't help noticing that she was not the center of his
attention. Nor was he, really, the center of hers. Not after the
banquet at *Conte* Visconti's estate. When her uncle had suggested that an engagement to the Cornaro boy, as he called
Marin, would be most beneficial, surely he hadn't anticipated
the *conte's* interest in his niece. She could tell the *conte* found
her upcoming engagement disagreeable, although he didn't say
it in so many words.

Anna had been looking for a way out without creating a scandal
or a vendetta. Her uncle was far too reluctant to make any move
out of fear of turning Andrea Cornaro into an enemy. Anna felt
like she was walking on a tight rope. As a first step, she would
procrastinate, she decided, but she didn't know what to do next.
She was relieved Marin was up to his ears with work and hon-
ored the custom of waiting until marriage before he made any
amorous advancement.

"No, but we bought the timber from the widow who owns this
place last spring." Marin looked at the deforested environs and
suspected that even more trees were cut than they had marked
that day. It was a sad, forsaken place that matched his dysphoria.

"Let's take a walk," Anna suggested, and they dismounted. "Is
this the widow's house?" Anna's gregarious nature found the silence between them horrendous.

Marin nodded and looked at their abandoned love nest with the wild mountain roses at the entrance in need of trimming.

"That must be some merry widow."

"What?" Anna's sarcastic comment startled him.

"Look, she's carrying someone's bastard."

Marin followed her gaze. His eyes came to rest on Elena who was having a hard time picking plums with her round belly, and his heart palpitated in his chest. Hippocrates barked and Elena turned and faced them. At the sight of Marin with his fiancé to be, her stomach churned, but she steeled herself against her nausea.

"Hippocrates, sit!" she cried out when the dog wanted to run to Marin.

Confused, Hippocrates stood still, looked at Elena, and then at Marin. "Sit!" Elena ordered again with a decisive voice, and the dog finally obeyed. Marin suppressed the urge to cuddle the half-breed.

Elena greeted them, and they walked up to her. When they were but a couple of paces away, Elena said, "*Signora*, mind your steps," and added coldly, "There are snakes around."

Anna let out a cry and hid her face on Marin's shoulder, failing to see the intense gaze between the two lovers. If Elena was alluding to the first day they met or implying that his behavior had been like a snakebite to her, Marin wasn't sure, and with Anna by his side his tongue was tied.

"How can you live here?" Appalled, Anna glanced around with insecurity.

"I don't any more, *signora*. You must be signor Zanetti's fiancé. Welcome to Cyprus," Elena said without bowing.

"Yes, thank you," Anna said and smiled for the first time since they had dismounted.

Elena observed the beautiful, tall, slender, rich Venetian lady who wouldn't let go of Marin's arm and felt short, fat, ugly, and insignificant.

"So where do you live now?" Marin asked with feverish eyes. He swiftly cast his gaze down on her belly and then back at her eyes, wearing an inquisitive look, but Elena's face was a courtesy mask.

"I have moved away, *signore*. That is why I'm afraid I'm unable to offer you anything but plums," she said evasively and offered them some fruit from her basket. Marin kept searching for her eyes, but Elena carefully focused her gaze on Anna who by now had forgotten her fear of snakes.

On their way back, Marin fell silent. He knew now beyond doubt he had to put an end to this charade of an engagement he had allowed himself to be fooled into. He might even know how...

78

2011

Marina walked to her car in brisk strides, eager to have some privacy for her racing thoughts. Her spirits were sinking fast, as she descended the hill and turned left toward Lemesos. She strictly forbade herself to speculate who the blonde was. It was simply none of her business. She told herself she was lucky she got off work earlier. She finally had the entire evening to herself. She could do whatever she wanted, starting with a bite to eat and a revision of her presentation. Then she might even call Katerina and arrange to go out.

Some forty minutes later, Marina closed the apartment door behind her and tossed her keys and her bag on the side table by the entrance. She ran her fingers through her hair and took a look around the familiar space that suddenly seemed suffocatingly small. She opened the fridge door, had a quick look at its disappointingly minimal and uninviting content and decided to skip dinner. She suppressed the urge to turn on her heels and disappear into the anonymity of the crowded commercial streets downtown. Instead, she turned on her laptop determined to focus on her thesis.

79

1468

The next morning, Marin was shown into *Conte* Visconti's office. Under different circumstances, Marin would have admired the opulent decor, but today he didn't even notice it. This was not a social call.

The *conte* rose from his seat and welcomed the dapper young man. "My dear Marin, what a lovely surprise!"

"Thank you for seeing me on such short notice, *conte*." Marin took the seat he was shown. His eyes rested for a moment on the deceased *contessa's* portrait on the wall behind the *conte's* desk.

"So what is the nature of the urgent matter you've come to see me about?"

The *conte* wondered if he had been too exuberant with Anna at the ball after all. He could only hope that Marin had not come to ask him to a duel. He knew too well he was no match for young, agile Marin.

"My fiancé *to be* is the cause of my visit, *conte*," Marin started carefully, noticing the bead of sweat that was formed on the *conte's* forehead.

"I hope everything's all right." The *conte* narrowed his eyebrows. He moved restlessly in his seat and wished this conversation was over already.

"It depends how you look at it, I suppose. *Conte*, may I be frank with you? My uncle has always spoken so highly of you, I feel I could confide in you," Marin said diplomatically.

"By all means, my dear boy." The *conte* tried hard to understand where this was leading and brought his handkerchief to his balding forehead.

"I fear that Anna is in love with you! Having seen the two of you alone on the balcony at your ball, I assume the same is true about you, too." Marin dropped his bomb and watched the *conte's* eyebrows rise and his eyes widen.

"Wha… What... what are you saying?" he stuttered.

"I'm saying that I fear I could never make her as happy as she would be by your side," he said now more subtly. "Therefore, I'm willing to swallow my pride and call off the engagement if I knew your intentions were honorable. I would hate to see her suffer, as I'm sure you would, too."

Marin folded his hands in tense anticipation. This was definitely the greatest social risk he had ever taken. He looked at the *conte* and cold sweat went down his spine when he realized that the discussion could end either way, but he kept his wits about him.

The *conte* examined the young man's face closely. Was this some kind of a prank, he wondered? The truth was that he was secretly in love with Anna, but such bold directness was unheard of. Yet Marin seemed sincere. He shifted in his seat a few more times, trying to stomach what he had just heard. What would be the young man's benefit to play a practical joke on him? The *conte* considered Marin's risk should he refuse.

"If I have your word as a gentleman, you have mine," the *conte* finally said, and the two men shook hands.

80

2011

At the reception the next morning, Marina asked the reception-ist to notify Mr. Zanetti of her arrival and waited for him in the lobby, mentally preparing for a long, difficult day.

When he joined her a few minutes later, he was wearing an in-scrutable expression. "Breakfast?" Lorenzo asked, not failing to notice the black circles around her eyes.

"Uh, no thanks," she said casually.

"Will you have a coffee, at least, with me?"

Why did he insist, she wondered? She nodded, and they took a seat at a nearby table and ordered two cappuccinos.

Lorenzo fixed his stare on her, trying to read her face and asked, "Why did you just up and leave last night?"

What? "Mr. Zanetti..."

"Lorenzo," he reminded her without smiling.

"I thought you didn't need me anymore."

"Last time I checked we were going to have dinner and celebrate my birthday together." His eyes were too solemn to look at, and Marina fixed her stare on the floor tile pattern.

"I thought you changed your mind."

What is this, she wondered? *I'm the one who should be upset here, not you*, she thought!

He studied her expressive face, and his voice was less grave when he spoke again.

"Help me understand this. When I left you at the bar, you were looking forward to spending the evening with me. Correct?"

She hesitated for a moment, and then she nodded.

"Why?"

Seriously? She cleared her throat. "It's obvious now that I was wrong, but I just had the impression that uh… we had a moment and uh…" she stopped at a loss for words. The corners of her mouth quirked upward.

"You were not wrong," he said quietly, and she met his gaze.

What kind of a game is this?

Lorenzo monitored her every reaction. She looked so young, so vulnerable.

"You were happy to spend the evening with me when you thought we had a moment, and you took off when Barbara showed up. Is that right?" he asked quietly.

Marina nodded and felt relieved when he made no attempt to continue this pointless conversation. They finished their coffee in silence and walked to the car where the porter was waiting with Lorenzo's luggage.

Marina raised her bewildered eyes to him. "You're cutting your stay short?"

"Just checking out. Will you open the car boot for the porter? He's waiting."

Marina unlocked the car trying hard to make sense. They got in, and she turned and locked eyes with him. "Where will you be staying?"

"I've already booked a room at the Four Seasons in Lemesos. You won't have to drive so much in the middle of the night."

"And Barbara?" She just couldn't resist the temptation.

He gave her an alluring smile. "Are you jealous?" he teased her and watched her swallow hard with amusement.

"She came all the way here just to see you – to spend your birthday with you." It still didn't add up exactly.

Lorenzo glanced out of the window and cleared his throat before turning to face her again. "About my birthday... It's actually on the twenty-third."

Marina shook her head in disbelief. "What? I don't get it. Why would you lie about it?"

"I did not exactly lie."

He noticed her lifted eyebrow and added. "Okay. It was a *white* lie. My birthday's just around the corner. What's the big difference? Besides, I feared you might not have accepted the dress otherwise, and I just wanted to make you a present. If it's that bad, I apologize."

Perplexed, Marina looked at his earnest expression and reminded herself she was no more than his private guide, and she should act like one. "I think it makes more sense to use the daylight for the excursion and leave the check in for later." She put on her professional shield once more.

"Marina!" He clasped her hand in his. "Barbara and I went out on a date once, and that's it. Nothing ever happened. Nothing ever will. If I'm checking out today, I'm doing it for you."

She stared into his Glaucous blue eyes for a fleeting moment before concentrating her gaze on her driving. "You are doing this *for me!*"

"Like I said before, you were right when you thought we had a moment. And I didn't want you to think there's anything going on between Barbara and me."

Marina remained reticent, contemplating the whole situation. Why should she believe anything he said? Didn't he lie to her about something as simple as his birthday?

Lorenzo looked at her pensively. She obviously needed more time, and time was a luxury he couldn't offer.

81

1468

After dinner, Marin invited Anna for a breath of fresh air in the garden. He knew there was no way of keeping what he had to tell her a secret from the servants, but he could do without an audience when he broke the news.

"It's a beautiful night," he started casually.

"Yes, it is." Anna tried to match his effort for polite conversation.

He led her to the bench underneath the honeysuckle. "Anna, you are the most beautiful woman I have ever seen." He had rehearsed what he would tell her. He would flatter her narcissistic nature and thirst for power and money.

"Thank you, Marin." Anna wondered what had gotten into him.

"You are educated and refined. You're every man's dream."

Just not mine, he thought and wondered if he was overdoing it with the flattery and decided to turn it down a bit.

"You have every right to happiness. You deserve more than a humble mill supervisor," he tried to break the news gently.

"What are you saying, Marin?" Anna wasn't sure she liked where he was going with it.

"I had a conversation with *Conte* Visconti today."

Anna raised her bewildered eyes to him, but Marin's face resembled the sphinx.

"What?"

"Did you know he's in love with you and that he wants to marry you?" Marin sounded almost accusingly.

"What?" Anna asked again at the loss for a better choice of words.

"I'm saying that I have noticed how happy the two of you looked together at the ball the other day. I would hate to be an obstacle in your way. Clearly, I could never be a match to what the *conte* has to offer you. So, I'm releasing you of our engagement. He's waiting for you."

Anna looked at him in astonishment. Could she be so lucky? "And you?"

"I will drown my pain in wine and work. At least, I will know that two out of the three of us will be happy."

Marin, you're a poet! Better still, you're a genius! Now, you need to find Elena and win her back, he thought. He feared that wouldn't be as easy as breaking off the engagement.

82

2011

They reached the charming Kakopetria village at the confluence of Garillis and Kargotis Rivers, parked the car in the new village, and took to ascending on foot the picturesque lane, as the entire old village is a pedestrian zone. Lorenzo took out his camera and took snapshots of the ladies selling their homemade sweets outside their houses, with the sloped tiled roofs and wooden balconies, at the sound of the two rivers flowing, before they stopped at the water mill for coffee.

Lorenzo glanced around at the beauty of this hidden-from-the-road coffee shop and studied her troubled face. "Marina, are we OK?"

"What?"

"You look... tense. Is it because of Barbara? What more can I do to prove to you that there's nothing going on between us?"

"You don't need to prove anything to me."

"But I want to, and I don't know what's going on it that little head of yours. Will you tell me?"

"It's nothing. I just..." Marina cast a glance around.

"Just what?" he asked patiently.

She finally met his gaze and said, "I just don't like lies. That's all."

He snorted. "Okay. Guilty as charged. Can I, at least, try and make it up to you?"

"What do you mean?"

"You'll see. Let's go back."

"Okay, but it's early for the 'Lemesos by night' tour you wanted to have."

"I know. I just want to pass by a food market or a supermarket."

"A food market?" she echoed his words.

"Yes. Let me redeem myself by cooking for you." He offered her a mischievous smile.

"What?"

"You heard me. I want to cook for you. Tonight."

"But where?" Marina asked alarmed.

"Surely there's a kitchen where you live."

"I must warn you. I don't really have a kitchen, just a kitchen niche."

"Don't worry. I'm sure it's perfect."

He was too charming to resist. "Okay," she finally consented and heard the violin ringtone of his cell.

"Good afternoon, your Grace... I see... I see. Thank you for your time and effort. I was wondering if it's possible to make a donation.... Thank you, your Grace. Goodbye."

"Well?"

"Well, it seems that the church records were destroyed when the Ottoman Turks looted and burnt down Christian churches once they had beaten the Venetians. The Latin Church even ceased to exist for ten years, until 1581, when it was reestablished, so the earliest documents date back to the end of the sixteenth century. The name Zanetti, especially Marin Zanetti, appears most frequently in the Famagusta District, but there is no direct link to the Marin Zanetti who was born in 1447, and it's impossible to tell with certainty if they are related."

"Are you disappointed?" she asked sympathetically.

"A bit. It's been a wild goose chase after all. I mean, I knew my chances to trace him were one in a billion, but I guess deep down I was hopeful. I don't regret my coming here though." He stared at her meaningfully.

Marina tilted her head to the side. "There might be one more lead," she said wearing a pensive face.

"Which is?"

"The Orthodox Church archives. For all we know, he might have married a Cypriot. It was not uncommon in mixed marriages to baptize some children Catholic and some Orthodox. We might be luckier there."

"How long do you think it will take?"

"I've no idea. My guess is that the archives are kept in the Archbishopric in Nicosia, but you have to follow a certain procedure to be allowed access to them, and I'm not so sure there's enough time to do it now... Perhaps you should initiate the search from Rovigo and plan another trip to Cyprus," she said with a cheeky smirk.

"Perhaps I should," he replied through half-closed eyes.

83

1468

With the engagement burden lifted off his shoulders, Marin felt like a new man. Not wanting to neglect his duties at the sugar mill or give Jacomo any bargaining chips over him, he discreetly entrusted Nikeforos to seek Elena out for him. Marin was hoping that the small size of the town and his sketches would lead to a quick result, but he was in for a big surprise. Nikeforos searched high and low day in day out, but Elena was nowhere to be found in or around Limassol.

"I'm sorry, Master Marin. Is there any other place she might have gone to?"

Nikeforos hated to let him down, and Marin's spirits were sinking rapidly.

"Your guess is as good as mine." Marin sighed.

"I'm just a simple man, Master Marin, but I'd say that if she's pregnant with another child in her arm, she can't have gone far."

Marin shrugged. "Continue the search in the direction of Paphos," he finally said and took a pouch full of sezins out of a drawer.

"Please, Master Marin. You are insulting me!"

Marin nodded apologetically.

"Don't worry, Master Marin. I will find her for you if that's the last thing I do." He could tell his master had become maniacally obsessed with finding her. He would probably do the same for Persephone, he thought.

Marin got on his horse and rode to their love nest and left her a message on the door. It read, "The engagement is off. I love you. Return to me, please!" It was a desperate move, but he was running out of ideas.

The days went by slowly without a word from Elena and without an encouraging word from Nikeforos. The thought that he drove her away from her own house in her condition was too much to stomach.

"Where are you, Elena? What have I done? What a fool I am! Oh, Nemesis, be merciful!"

84

2011

They carried the shopping bags into the kitchen niche, and Marina gave Lorenzo a ten-second tour of the apartment.

"Venice!" he said happily surprised when his eyes rested on the poster on the wall.

Marina shoved her hands in the pockets of her chino pants. "Yeah, ever since I was a kid, I've always wanted to go to Venice. I'd like to travel all over the world one day, but Venice... How can I explain this? It's not exactly a déjà vu. It's more of a gut feeling that I have to go there one day."

"When you do, look me up," he said and handed her his business card. "I'd love to show you around. I can be your private guide for a change."

An electrifying silence followed their smiles.

"Okay, chef. How can I help?" Marina broke the silence.

"You've done enough. You've been driving and explaining all day. Why don't you have a shower and let me worry about dinner? Off you go now. I don't want you tired for our 'Lemesos by night' tour." He gestured for her to make him space in the kitchen.

Marina took her old white-washed jeans and a fitted top, her usual home outfit, out of the closet and disappeared into the shower, while Lorenzo made sure his cell was on silent mode. Marina took her clothes off and was about to turn the tap when she stood still straining her ears. She snorted when she heard Lorenzo singing *La Donna è Mobile*, visualizing him over his pots and pans, keeping the rhythm with his ladle.

85

1468

On some pretext, Marin left the mill early right after Nikeforos informed him of Elena's whereabouts and rode toward Paphos with the wind in his face and his brain overflowing with questions. Would she have him back? Why did she disappear? Was there anyone else? Was that his baby? Was there a future for them? What would he say to his uncle? What options did he have if his uncle opposed their wedding?

He followed Nikeforos's instructions. He rode along the coast and turned right before the castle, all the way up to the Catacombs. It was the last mud-brick house right before the Catacombs. He dismounted and tied his horse safely. He walked the few steps to her dwelling, with his heart on the verge of bursting in his chest as adrenaline reached a new high. He smoothed his hair, took a deep breath and finally knocked on her door.

Elena opened the door unable to utter a word.

"Ma…in," Ioanna shouted excitedly as she appeared right behind her mother. She rushed with staggering steps toward him.

Marin went down on his knees, opened his arms for her to hide in, lifted her up, and tossed her in the air. "Look at you! You can walk and talk already!" He gave her a squeezing hug, closed his eyes, and filled her head with little kisses.

Hippocrates, who came to see what the commotion was all about, woofed around him demanding his attention. With Ioanna in his left arm, Marin stretched his right arm and patted Hippocrates playfully while Elena watched unable to move.

Was that really him? How did he find her? *Breathe*, she reminded herself.

"She's grown!" Marin stated the obvious.

Yeah, you missed that while you were having fun with your fiancé, Elena thought wryly. "What are you doing here?" she asked austerely when she finally was in command of her voice again.

"Elena, we need to talk. Aren't you going to ask me to come in?" He half-feared she wouldn't.

Elena hesitated for a moment but decided she could do without the neighbors' gossip and let him in. Marin had a quick glance around at her humble place and took the seat she offered him.

She sat opposite him and folded her arms in front of her chest. "I'm listening," Elena encouraged him although she wasn't sure she wanted to hear what he had to say.

With Ioanna on his lap and Hippocrates at his feet, Marin looked deeply into Elena's eyes, took a piece of paper out of his doublet, and asked the question he had so long waited for to ask, "Why?"

Her eyes focused on the note she had left for him on the door of nana's house and decided not to satisfy his curiosity. She lifted her chin and looked him straight in the eye.

"Don't you think I'm the one who should be asking this question?"

86

2011

Marina took her time under the steaming water, striving to put her thoughts in order. When she joined him again, he was adding the final touches. Lorenzo stopped what he was doing and looked at her from head to toe - her hair still damp and no make-up.

"Do you have an ID?" The seriousness in his voice startled her.

"What?"

"I could swear you look seventeen right now." His penetrating gaze caused her heart to thump.

"Is that bad?"

"No, unless you are. Then I'm in trouble!" He chuckled.

"Why?" she asked, trying to wipe the self-satisfied grin off her face.

Lorenzo lit the candle on the table, poured some wine in two glasses, and offered her one.

"You know why," he said boldly. He clinked his glass against hers. Slowly, he pinched a prawn-smoked-salmon saffron ravioli, one of Lorenzo's signature dishes, with his fork. "Here, try this."

Marina closed her eyes and concentrated on the tantalizing taste sensation. "Mm... Mm... this is so delectably scrumptious – divine!" The rapture on her face was what he had craved.

He pulled her close and felt her heart racing as he brushed his lips playfully against hers taking his time. She clasped his neck and responded with a delirious lingering kiss that took them both by surprise, awakening senses and reflexes.

"*Amore mio,*" he whispered short of breath. He hid his face in the curls on her neck, kissing her, tasting her like a Château Lafitte. Marina surrendered to the magic of his kiss and the seductive sound of Italian words of love he whispered in her ear. "*Sei tanto bella… carissima…*"

The ringing of the doorbell put an abrupt end to their moment.

"Expecting someone?" he asked, holding her in his arms still.

"No. They'll go away."

But the ringing became more persistent.

87

1468

"You haven't been back to our love nest, have you?" Marin enquired without answering her question - their eyes still locked.

Love nest! "No."

"I left you a note there explaining there's not going to be an engagement." He stared at her with his penetrating Glaucous blue eyes.

He obviously expected her to ask 'why', but she wouldn't grant him this satisfaction, although she was dying to find out. She felt something stirring inside her and clenched her stomach. *Oh, you can stop kicking now*, she thought!

"Elena, are you all right?"

She looked up and met his worried look. "Other than you broke my heart to pieces, I am the size of an elephant, and I have to raise the children all by myself... yeah, I'd say everything's fine." She rose to her feet. "I have to check on the food."

She didn't really. She had just added the *trahanas*[1] into some boiling water when she heard him knock on the door, but she needed an excuse to put some physical distance between them. She needed time to think. But Marin could read her face like the palm of his hand. He followed her to the boiling cauldron, let Ioanna down on her blanket, and gave her a *puppa*[2]. Ioanna took it, put it in her mouth, and rubbed it against her sore gums.

"Need a hand?" he asked casually as if nothing had changed between them. He came and stood right behind her.

---

1 Cracked wheat and soured goat's milk.

2 A doll made of rugs - from French puppée.

Elena felt flustered. Why wouldn't he leave her be for a moment? "No, thank you," she said and stood with her back still turned to him, avoiding his gaze that was so upsetting.

"You think you have stirred the food long enough?" he asked gently.

Elena took a deep breath, mastered her self-control, and turned to face him. "What do you want, Marin?" She emphasized every single word. The proximity of his body agitated the balance of her pregnancy hormones even more. Why was he doing this to her?

"You and Ioanna in my life," he whispered in her ear, sending thrills to her excited body and mind.

Pull yourself together! He abandoned you first chance he had, she reminded herself.

"You did have us in your life. Apparently, we have failed to fulfill your needs." The bitterness in her voice felt like a slap on his face.

"You haven't failed me, Elena. I have." His voice was hoarse.

"Yes, you have. You... you cheated on me!"

"I did not. I never touched her."

Elena looked at him through narrowed eyes, wondering if he was telling the truth. "Still, you were going to get engaged to her."

"But I never did," he said in a quiet tone of voice that infuriated her even more.

"You... You did not respect me... You..." Noticing Ioanna's puzzled look, she took a deep breath to calm herself.

"I have always had the greatest respect for you," Marin said quietly, but Elena cut him short.

"You call this respect!" she cried out indignantly.

"That was the most stupid mistake in my entire life! Elena, I'm sorry. I'm truly sorry I hurt you. Let me make it up to you."

His pleading eyes met hers, but Elena had no intention of making it easy on him.

"For how long? Until another puffed and powdered fancy lady hits your way? Face it, Marin. We live in two different worlds you and I. I carry the stigma of a common native and can never be part of your life with the exquisite banquets and feasts." Her voice was a farrago of resolve and acrimony.

"Elena, I won't lie to you. It is a tempting world, but it means nothing without you. Trust me. I've been there. I know now."

88

2011

"Maybe you should get that," Lorenzo said without smiling and let go of her.

Marina stepped away from him and ran her fingers through her hair. Ill-equipped for the intensity of the emotions his kiss had evoked in her, she stood with her hand on the door knob for a few moments, only too aware that his eyes were fixed on her.

She took a deep breath and straightened her shoulders before she opened the door. A clean-shaven George in a navy blue suit, white shirt, and blue and yellow tie stood half-hidden behind a bouquet of red roses.

Still standing in the kitchen niche, Lorenzo scrutinized Marina's perplexed expression and heard the young man's wheedling voice until his olive green eyes rested on him.

So, you're the lover boy, Lorenzo thought.

The young man's voice became cold as ice when he spoke again. He must have asked Marina who Lorenzo was because Marina made the introductions in English in an attempt to keep this awkward situation as civil as possible.

Lorenzo humored her, came closer, and stretched his arm, but George ignored him. He turned to Marina and spoke fervently, but she spoke in a quiet, almost tender voice. Eventually, the young man nodded and cast a glance at Lorenzo who could not fathom from their facial expressions or their tone of voice what was going on exactly and that irritated him. His flexed muscles relaxed only when Marina closed the door behind the young man moments later.

Marina stood with her forehead against the door for a while. Lorenzo didn't move, sensing she needed time and space.

89

1468

"Trust you! I've already done that. I can't say I'm impressed," Elena said disdainfully.

Marin sighed. He was running out of ideas. He only knew he didn't want to lose her again. "Elena, please, I don't want to live without you. I love you. I want to spend the rest of my life with you."

"Like master and mistress?" she asked with contempt.

He looked at her intensely and said in a gruff voice, "Like my wife." He got down on one knee and asked, "Will you marry me?"

"What would your uncle say?" Elena challenged him.

Marin didn't miss the provocative touch in her voice. She had every right to be hurt and chagrined, he reminded himself. He placed his palms on her belly, kissed it, and rose to his feet.

"Let me worry about that. You just worry about the children. How pregnant are you anyway?"

"The baby's due in two new moons."

Marin made a quick calculation in his mind. "Let me be there for you and the children. For their sake," he added tenderly.

Elena's pride wanted to hurt him as much as he had hurt her, but it would only be a fleeting moment of her ego's victory to tell him to go. She looked at his earnest expression.

"If I were to allow you to visit us, could you live in celibacy for as long as it takes?" she challenged him with a draconian measure, knowing his Achilles' heel only too well.

"If that's what you *really* want."

"I swear to you, Marin, if I hear the slightest gossip about you and prostitutes even, I'll move somewhere you will never find me or your child," she threatened, her icy tone of voice serious as a heart attack, but Marin chose to pay attention to the words that interested him the most.

"So it *is* mine!" He smiled at her affectionately and placed his palms gently on her rounded belly.

"Whose did you think it was?" she asked affronted.

"Mine, but it's still nice to hear it from your lips." He felt the tenderness for her and his unborn child welling inside him.

He bent down to kiss her, but she turned her face away. "I don't remember saying I forgave you. You will clear your position with your uncle first. When is your next report to him?"

"In less than a fortnight."

"Come and see me then." She turned to stir the soup, implying his time was up.

He came and stood right behind her again. "Elena!" His husky whisper in her ear always worked, and he knew it when she got the goose bumps.

"What?"

What a pyrrhic victory! She was regretting the celibacy condition already.

"You are even more beautiful when you are pregnant. And I could swear your breasts are larger... When I'm forgiven, we should do this more often. I want to have a house full of children with you."

"Provided I forgive you and you stay around long enough."

"I will. You'll see."

90

2011

"Do you mind if we skip the 'Lemesos by night' tour tonight? I'd rather drive you to the hotel now if that's all right with you." Her voice trailed off.

"Sure. No problem," he lied. He locked eyes with her, but Marina did not even want to try and make out his inscrutable gaze. She had to put her own thoughts in order first.

On the illuminated coastal road, Marina turned left and headed east toward Germasogeia and the Four Seasons Hotel. There was hardly any traffic that January Thursday night, but Marina drove unusually slowly with her vacant gaze fixed on the road. Lorenzo frowned and rubbed his chin, squeezing his brain for a way to bring down the glass wall she erected withdrawing in her silence. For lack of any smart ideas, he remained quiet, too.

When Marina pulled up by the hotel entrance, Lorenzo knew it was a long shot, but he gave it a try anyway.

"Would you like to come in for a drink? Perhaps talk about what happened tonight? You may not know this about me, but I'm an excellent listener... Or not talk at all. You don't have to go through this alone, you know. I'm here for you."

"Thanks, but it's late... Do you think you could check in alone?"

He nodded faking a smile.

"Same time tomorrow?"

"Sure. You can call me any time. Good night." Lorenzo gave her a quick kiss on the cheek and got out of the car.

91

1468

"That was reckless." Andrea Cornaro took his spectacles off and placed them on a pile of documents on his desk, as soon as Marin finished reporting on the sugar mill and the cotton farm progress.

"I beg your pardon?"

"Arranging Anna's engagement with Visconti. You do realize this could have ended in a vendetta."

But it didn't, the young man contemplated but held his tongue.

"That would have been an egregious error. You acted irresponsibly, Marin." Andrea was disappointed in Marin for the first time.

"The *conte* is happy, Anna is happy, the Contarini are happy. I'm happy. So, what's the problem? I don't love her, uncle," Marin said to his defense.

"What has love got to do with marriage? You'd learn to love her along the way. She's young, beautiful, educated, and rich. What's there not to love?"

Marin wondered if his uncle had ever loved a woman like he loved Elena, but he decided not to go down that path. "Well, it's over now."

"What do you intend to do with this native? I hear she's pregnant. Is this your child?" Andrea studied Marin's face.

Marin wondered how his uncle knew. Yet again, he wondered if there was anything going on on this island that he didn't know of. "Yes, Sir."

"What do you want to do?" Andrea folded his hands on the desk in front of him.

Marin swallowed hard. "Marry her, with your permission."

"My permission! You didn't ask for my permission when you broke off the engagement… Marin, this woman is no match for you. She has nothing to offer you. You can do great things, my boy. I've seen how your brain works. Married into the right family, you could do wonders, but you'll have an insignificant, isolated life in poverty with her. Why? Because you love her? What makes you so sure your love won't wither?"

He snorted scornfully and went on, "Love… If you loved her – if you really loved her like you think you do – how come you agreed to marry Anna, Marin?"

"That was a temporary erosion of judgment." How many times did he have to apologize for the same mistake?

"So you say now. What will you do in a few years' time when your love for the widow is stilled and the misery of your new life dawns on you, and more beautiful young ladies come your way? What makes you so sure that romantic love guarantees a successful marriage?"

"I would like to try anyway." Marin tried not to get upset with his uncle for whom he had the greatest respect.

Seeing the young man's determination, Andrea looked at him with renewed interest. Was he really willing to lose it all? He decided to change his tactics.

"Marin, why don't you wait a while with this marriage idea?" *Why buy the cow when you can milk it?* "I'm throwing a banquet at my residence in Nicosia next Saturday. This is an opportunity to meet more ladies. Humor me, Marin; do this for me!" he said, making a mental note to assign his secretary to organize a banquet right after Marin left.

"All right, uncle. I will respect your wish and keep my eyes open for the woman who will steal my heart from Elena's hands. But if no one does, I expect your blessings at our wedding."

"As long as you promise to keep an open mind," Andrea said and realized he needed to come up with a backup plan.

92

2011

Lorenzo awoke with the memory of the sensation of the kiss the night before and had a hard time controlling his imagination and his testosterone. But the warm smile that lit her eyes and drew him to her was hardly there that morning, he noticed with disappointment.

"Originally, I had thought of a trip to Pafos for your last day — it is so archaeologically abundant that the entire town is on the UNESCO World Heritage List, but since we only have a few hours before your flight, we should perhaps best visit Kourion. It's just a thirty-minute drive," she suggested wearing her professional smile that fortified the glass wall between them.

"Exactly because these are my last few hours here, I just want to spend them with you."

He looked at her intensely, but Marina cast her gaze on her hands.

"So what would *you* like to do?" Lorenzo took her hand in his, but she pulled it gently away and picked up her coffee cup.

"Visit Kourion. You'll love it." Her voice was professionally polite.

"Then Kourion it is." Lorenzo sighed somewhat miffed.

Some forty-five minutes later, they were walking on the bridge over the well-preserved mosaics in the complex of Eustolios at Kourion. Lorenzo heard Marina's voice explaining something about the image symbolism, but he wasn't really listening. Had George sweet-talked her after all? Did it matter? Lorenzo was unprepared for the cold shoulder she was giving him or how it gave his ulcer an anxiety attack. She must have grown on him while he wasn't paying attention, he thought.

He followed her to the stage of the impressive fully-restored Greco-Roman amphitheater with the panoramic view of the Mediterranean. Marina was now explaining how the amphitheater seats some two thousand spectators and how several cultural events still take place there today, but he stood still and Marina stopped talking. She turned and saw him leaning indolently against the wall – his weight on one foot.

"Do we have a problem, *amore mio?*"

He deliberately used the words of love he told her the night before, so that she knew exactly what he was heading at. Marina fixed her eyes on the restless waves wordlessly.

He shoved his hands into his pockets. "Why are you avoiding me?"

Silence. For an articulate person, Marina had absolutely no idea how to go about expressing her feelings and thoughts.

"Have I done anything to offend you?" he tried again.

"No, everything's fine." That was a flat lie, and they both knew it.

"Correct me if I'm wrong, but I thought we had a spark last night," he said carefully.

"You could say that," Marina said still not looking at him.

"And if we hadn't been interrupted, there might have been even more?"

"Perhaps. So?" She shrugged.

"So, you don't turn people on, and then drive them away. Why are you so distant today?"

Marina tore her gaze away from the rough sea and looked into his Glaucous blue eyes. "What do you want from me, Lorenzo? You are leaving in a few hours." She puckered her brows.

"Is that the only reason why you're so distant?" So George had nothing to do with it? Lorenzo felt relief to see her shrug and nod, while Marina wondered what difference it made. It was an impossible love – period.

It was a silent drive back to the hotel. Lorenzo wondered what she might have told George that pacified him and made him leave but refrained from asking.

93

1468

Having waited in tense anticipation, Elena thought her heart would burst when Marin finally showed up at her doorstep several days later.

He took her by the hand and led her to the sofa. "Elena," he looked at her searching for the right words.

She stared at him with her almond-shaped brown eyes, unable to control her curiosity. "Well? What did your uncle say? Has he given you his blessing?"

Marin's jaw stiffened and Elena knew the news couldn't be good.

"Not exactly," he started carefully, and Elena's eyebrows furrowed into an inquisitive look. "He's not against it. He just thinks I should not rush into anything," he added.

Elena could see that his uncle's pharisaic olive branch was not more than a Trojan horse. Most likely he needed time for his plan to keep them apart.

"Exactly, how long does your uncle think it's appropriate to wait?" she asked, trying to measure her words, knowing of the high esteem Marin had for his uncle

"He wasn't that specific, but we should wait a while," he said vaguely.

Elena took a deep breath and mastered all her patience, a rather difficult task with her upset pregnancy hormones.

"I'll be having your child soon, Marin. Do you wish your son to be born outside of wedlock?"

"My son? How do you know it's a boy?" Marin avoided the real question.

"Because my pregnancy is different this time. Do you wish your child to be born a *bastard*?" Elena insisted.

"Elena, what's eating you? I'm not your grandfather or your father! I do want to marry you. I will marry you."

"You do see that I'm the one in a vulnerable position here."

"You do see that I'm the one risking everything here!" The words slipped out.

"Is this what I am for you, Marin? *A risk*?" Her eyes narrowed dangerously.

"Don't go down that path, Elena. If I go against my uncle's wishes, I lose everything."

"*Everything?*" She folded her arms in front of her chest.

Marin put his hands on her shoulders.

"Listen! Listen to me! I never want to lose you again. If I had to choose, of course, I would choose you over my uncle. I just hope it won't come to that. I know I'm asking for too much right now, but you will have to trust me. Let me deal with this. I think I may know how."

Elena lost herself in those blue eyes. With her growing belly, she felt more vulnerable with each passing day. Even if he chose her over his uncle, would he not regret it, she wondered?

94

2011

"Would you like to come up to my room for a drink while I pack?" Lorenzo asked casually when they got back to the hotel.

"Uh... I think I better wait for you here," Marina said quietly, avoiding his gaze.

"Sure." The corners of his mouth twitched as he pushed the elevator button and watched her walk to the lobby.

Marina ordered a coffee and sat by the large French windows overlooking the patio with the charming wooden bridges over the little ponds, lost in her thoughts. She almost didn't hear her cell phone ring.

"Hey, Katerina."

"Someone's carrying the world on her shoulders," Katerina observed perceptively.

Marina sighed. "Nothing as tragic as that."

"Okay, what's wrong?"

"I'm in love and he's packing," Marina gave her the abridged version.

"The Italian client?"

Marina nodded. "The very same."

"What do you want to do?"

"Nothing. What's there to do? He's a client. And he's leaving."

Katerina was silent for a moment, and then she asked, "Is this mutual?"

"I don't know. For all I know, it's just a holiday fling for him."

"Want me to pass by?"

"No, it's okay. I have to drive him to the airport anyway."

"Hang in there, Marina *mou*. Call me when you get back."

"Sure." Marina hung up and took a sip of her coffee absent-mindedly.

95

1468

In the next few weeks, Andrea Cornaro arranged for Marin to attend one social event after another and on various pretexts, he required his presence in the capital. In an effort not to alarm Elena, Marin tried to conceal his frequent outings from her. To distract her attention, he even ordered a long, white, silk dress, with an embroidered rim that could even be used as a wedding dress.

"This is for you. It's from Venice," he said when he presented her with his gift when they next met.

"If I can fit into it," Elena said, looking at the dress unenthusiastically.

Marin observed the there's-something-wrong-but-I-won't-tell-you-what expression on her face.

"Elena, is everything all right?"

"Yes! Lunch is ready," she said and took to serving the honey-crusted roasted lamb with spinach, peeled almonds, and raisins.

"It's delicious," Marin said, hoping to lift her spirits, but Elena just offered him a faint smile.

"The baby could come any day now, Marin," she said after a while.

Marin wasn't sure he could read her eyes. "That's terrific. I can't wait."

"And you still want to marry me?" she asked quietly.

"You know I do. You just have to be a bit more patient."

Elena took her time looking him in the eye before she spoke again. "A Venetian gentleman paid me a visit this last week."

"What gentleman?" Marin asked suspiciously. "What did he want?"

"He wanted to help me understand that if I really loved you, I should set you free. As if I ever owned you in any way! Apparently, I'm ruining your career prospects and your social status. I think his exact words were 'I'm dragging you down to my abyss.' He even offered me money if I were to leave Paphos and disappear from your life."

Marin was trying to deduce what was going on. "What did you say?" he asked quietly, but his mind was racing.

"That the baby is due any day now and even if I wanted to, it is impossible to leave straightaway, and I asked him if his offer would still be valid until after I gave birth." There! She said it. It was off her chest now.

"You mean you are *thinking* about it?" After he had called off the engagement to the Contarini girl for her? Marin's eyebrows furrowed in an inquisitive look, and then he frowned in disbelief.

"I mean, I bought us, or me, time. He didn't exactly threaten me in so many words, but the threat was in the air all right. If you want to marry me, as you say you do, now is the time. If you don't, I still need to think about Ioanna and the new baby. I can't allow anything to happen to me. Do you understand the gravity of my situation, Marin, while you are having fun at the balls your uncle sends you to?" she asked reproachfully.

Marin gnashed his teeth and clenched his fist irately. "Would you be in any position to travel if necessary?"

"If I have to travel, the sooner the better." Elena wondered what was going on in his head, but it was impossible to tell.

They finished their lunch in silence. When Marin got ready to leave, he put his arms around her and said, "You'll hear from me before Sunday. I need to clear out a few things. I'll be back for you. All of you."

Marin rode back to Episkopi, chasing the thought away that Elena was playing him against Andrea. He found it hard to stomach that his uncle would finagle his way into separating him from Elena. He was almost certain that the gentleman who had paid her a visit was Jacomo but thought it wiser not to confront him. If that were the case, he was only acting upon Andrea's instructions.

Marin quickly assessed the situation. He had put aside enough to get them a house and make a fresh start. By now, he had established a network of associates and business acquaintances that might be useful in starting up his own business, preferably dealing with spices like he had done before he came to Cyprus - provided he wouldn't ignite his uncle's wrath.

96

2011

Lorenzo's steps were unusually slow as he walked to the car. He placed his suitcase in the car boot and sat in the passenger seat.

"I was thinking I should follow that lead you gave me about the Orthodox Church," he said when Marina shifted into reverse and pulled out of the parking lot.

"Perhaps you should," she replied quietly and steered the car onto the coastal road.

"I'd like to come back for a longer vacation in the summer time - with Paola. I bet it's more beautiful then."

Marina looked at him sideways, wondering if he was just making polite conversation. "It's definitely warmer."

"How about you? Any plans of finally visiting Venice any time soon? I'd love to show you around."

Marina wondered if he was looking for a pen friend or a long-distance relationship. She knew she was interested in neither. Those were merely alternatives to postponing the inevitable.

"One day. I'll need to get a job first," she said evasively.

Lorenzo scrutinized her guarded expression, and drawing upon his finest command of language, he remained silent.

97

1468

At the first streaks of dawn, Marin set off to Nicosia, but he found he had to wait a couple of hours before he was finally let into the office of the Auditor of the Kingdom, as Andrea had been caught up in a lengthy meeting with the king.

"Marin, I'm sorry I kept you waiting so long," Andrea said with a smile on his face, but Marin could tell from the dark circles around his eyes that he must have had a sleepless night.

"It's all right. I had the chance to collect my thoughts in the peace of the palace gardens."

"That sounds serious." Andrea concentrated his attention on the young man. He had the gift of focusing on a situation completely in spite of what else might be on his mind.

"Uncle, I know you are extremely busy and perhaps today is not the best of days to distract you from your work with my personal problems, but I will only take a few minutes of your time."

"What seems to be the problem?" Andrea took off his spectacles and rubbed the bridge of his nose.

"I hope you see how hard I have worked for you since the day I set foot on this island," Marin said, seeking to establish common ground.

"You know I do," Andrea encouraged him.

"I have always done what you asked of me." Andrea nodded, and Marin went on. "Uncle, I've come for your blessing to marry Elena."

The die had been cast.

Andrea folded his hands and said contemplatively, "I take it that no young lady has managed to steal your heart away."

"I'm afraid not," Marin replied steadfastly.

"I was hoping we wouldn't have to have this conversation... Do you know that the widow is willing to walk away from you for the right price?" Andrea examined the young man's face.

"So it is true! You did send someone." Marin sounded disappointed and bitter. He was half hoping Elena's story was fabricated.

"I have underestimated her," Andrea said quietly. "She's more devious than I thought. Beware of her, Marin," he warned the young man. "Think! Why would she tell you? She wants to look like the victim here, but make no mistake, Marin. She was more than willing to take the money." Andrea's rebuking gaze bore into the young man's eyes, but the latter didn't flinch.

Marin had mentally prepared for anything. He had nothing to gain from a conflict with his uncle. "I have come for your blessing, uncle, like you promised," he said, focusing on the crux of the matter and keeping his voice steady and low.

"Can't you see it's the money she's after? Open your eyes, Marin! You have a future full of prospect ahead of you. Don't waste it on an ignorant native!" Andrea said disdainfully.

Marin decided not to dignify that with an answer. "Am I to understand you will not give me your blessings as *promised*?"

Marin wouldn't take the bait, and Andrea had no other cards to play. "I wish I could, my boy. Believe me. I wish I could." Andrea suddenly looked much older.

"In that case, I must bid you farewell. I'm afraid our paths part here. It's been an honor to serve you, but now I need to look after my family. I will always be at your service anyway I can." One of the principles of human conduct his father had taught him was to avoid burning bridges whenever possible.

"You are leaving!" Andrea could hardly hide his astonishment and his defeat.

"I'm afraid so. I don't see how I can stay without your blessing, and marry Elena I shall." Marin rose to his feet.

"Where will you be going?" Andrea asked wearily.

"Famagusta. I have some money of my own. I could trade in spices. I know a few things about that. We'll be all right."

"Famagusta! Perhaps you should get in touch with Francisco da Lucca. I'll send word."

Andrea called his secretary into his office and whispered something in his ear. The young man left quietly only to return with a pouch a couple of minutes later. When he closed the door behind him, Andrea walked up to Marin and extended his arm with the pouch.

"Consider this as my wedding gift to you."

The two men embraced and locked eyes in an eloquent gaze.

98

2011

The car came to a complete stop outside the departing flights area. Marina grabbed her bag, took out an ash grey box, and handed it to him. She mastered all her strength, put a smile on her face, and said, "This is for you."

"Thank you!" Lorenzo untied the indigo ribbon and opened the box she offered him. "A silver pomegranate! Does it symbolize anything?"

"Cypriots believe it brings good luck. It was also one of Aphrodite's symbols – a symbol of love."

She cast her gaze to the pomegranate and refrained from explaining that it was also a symbol of the consummation of marriage and fertility.

Lorenzo searched her eyes. Was she saying she loved him? He planted a kiss on her forehead and thanked her for her gift. He had this vague feeling that he had to do or say something, but he wasn't sure what.

Marina walked him to his counter, and Lorenzo checked his suitcase in and came to stand close to her. He looked at the clock on the wall, aware that these were their last minutes together. Their eyes locked in silence. He scratched the back of his head and cast his gaze down at his shoes.

"You know... I have a daughter and a business to go back to, but perhaps you…" He cast a glance around and shoved his hands in his pockets.

Marina held him in a quizzical look. "I... what?"

"I was just thinking that... perhaps you could... uh... could take a break after your defense to... uh…"

"To do what?" Marina searched his eyes.

He gave her an exaggerated grimace. "Oh, I don't know. You might want to come and visit Venice - or me," he finally said with a cheeky smirk.

"Exactly, what are you saying?" Marina dare not hope.

"We could give it a try - you and I. What do you say?" His Glaucous blue eyes sank into hers.

She looked at him through half-closed eyes, her heart beating like crazy. "We could, I guess," she said quietly, trying to grasp what she was agreeing to.

"Yes?" he asked for confirmation.

"Yes," she nodded and gave him a wide smile.

He took her in his arms, and for what seemed like an eternity, they lost themselves in an embrace, oblivious to the people around them.

"This is the final call for passenger Costas Constantinou on flight CY326 to London Heathrow. Please proceed to the boarding gate immediately," a strict voice announced.

As if awoken from lethargy, they cut off their embrace. Lorenzo looked at her unable to resist the temptation after all.

"What did you tell George last night that made him walk away just like that?"

She snorted. "Does it matter?"

"Not really. I'm just curious."

"I told him the truth."

"Which is?" he asked patiently.

"That I'm in love with you."

He bent down and took her lips in a sweet kiss one last time.

99

1468

The next few months passed quickly for Marin and his new wife. Moving to Famagusta, opening a house there, giving birth, embarking on a new career, and looking after three babies absorbed all of their time. They named the twins Alexandro, after Marin's father, and Guglielmo, after Elena's father, according to the custom of naming the children after their grandparents.

Marin's business prospered, and soon he was able to buy his parents a vast estate about eighty kilometers southwest of Venice to encourage his father to retire. Marin and Elena had seven more children, five boys and two girls, one of which did not survive the great epidemic that broke out in 1470. A year later, one of the boys was lost in the catastrophic earthquake.

Andrea Cornaro's endeavors finally paid off. Caterina Cornaro was married to James II by proxy, in 1468, in Venice. She arrived on the island four years later and was crowned Queen of Cyprus. Andrea came to Famagusta to pay Marin and his wife a visit and apologize to Elena who had just given birth to another healthy boy that they named Andrea after him. Andrea paid them a couple more visits before he was accused of poisoning the king and kidnapping his son on behalf of the *Serenissima*. Murdered in 1473, he never saw the flags of the Republic of San Marco rise in 1489, which signalized the abolition of the kingdom of Cyprus.

ABOUT THE AUTHOR

LINA ELLINA

Lina Ellina has worked as a lecturer at
the University of Trier in Germany and at
Intercollege in Cyprus as well as a business
consultant. Together with her husband, she
has created and run their company in Anogyra
specializing in organic olive oil.

At various stages, Lina's interest included sports,
music, painting, reading, and theater. Today
she's more into history, culture, food and wine.